ACE CARROWAY
AND THE
GREAT WAR

GUY WORTHEY

ACE CARROWAY AND THE GREAT WAR

This is a work of fiction. Names, characters, places, and incidents are either the product of the author's imagination or are used fictitiously. Any resemblance to actual persons, living or dead, is entirely coincidental.

Cover design: Ioana Ramona Cecalasan

ISBN: 1976482399
ISBN-13: 978-1976482397

Westing Press

To my mother. Tall. Strong. Smart. Loved.

The Times

ILLUSTRATED DAILY NEWSPAPER

Price 5p

AIR RAIDS INTENSIFY

More powerful bombs fall on London.

Three neighbourhoods' were damaged in Thursday's air raids, entirely demolishing at least three buildings. Five civilians are known to have perished, and 17 others were injured. R.A.F. spokesman B. J. Littleton said the bombs were dropped from "heavy aircraft" and speculated that the planes originated from "captured areas of Belgium." Mr. Littleton did not respond to questions about whether the R.A.F. French fleet should be brought home to protect

Bomb shelters overcrowded.

Even the newly constructed bunkers were overrun during the raid, causing considerable distress amongst those seeking shelter. Part of this may be due to the completion of the air raid siren array, according to construction engineer H. Thorpe Norris. He speculates that more people were aware of the raid, and sought shelter

Roads cleared. Fires smoulder.

Civil authorities urge due

Soissons Lost.

Bad news from France did little to lighten the mood. The P.M. confirmed yesterday's reports that Ottoman forces swept through Allied forces in and near Soissons, France. The loss brings more territory under Ottoman control, including farms, several factories and a key airstrip. British Army spokesman Maj. G. Collins, however, was upbeat. "There are bound to be hiccups," he said, "but soon we'll have the American Expeditionary smoothly integrated with the British Regulars."

Chapter 1

Incoming bullets chipped wood and frayed fabric in the wings and body of the SPAD biplane in a muted pitter-patter of death. The Allied pilot barrel-rolled the biplane left. But it was a feint. The SPAD peeled out of the roll, rose sharply up, and looped backwards and upside down.

The enemy pilot cursed when he realized he had not hit anything vital. He cursed again when his quarry soared above him. He tried to follow, but the airspeed of his Eindecker monoplane dropped. He almost stalled. For a few seconds, he slowly tipped over into a dive, knowing he was easy prey for the SPAD. He expected bullets to fly and end it. The SPAD passed by, its engine buzzing loud in the cold air. No bullets flew, but something heavy struck the edge of his cockpit and clattered downwards into the pedals.

He glanced incredulously at the SPAD. The Allied pilot, in leather cap and goggles, gave him a two-fingered salute. The momentary eye contact contained no hatred, only solemn respect focused by the iron clench of a resolute jaw. And she was a woman! The enemy pilot's eyes followed the biplane as it banked away into the sunset.

He shook off his stupor and looked down to his feet. Between the rudder pedals lay the tubular shape of an Allied grenade! He frantically reached for it, but it was too late. The next second, his plane was a fireball.

The Allied fighter roared home. It was a French-built SPAD[1], a wood frame covered in glue-soaked fabric. An aileron cable had been cut by a bullet. The pilot compensated for the broken aileron with the elevators and landed with deceptive ease. The ground crew ran to meet the plane as it rolled toward the hangar. The pilot killed its engine. The crew threw chocks under the wheels and rolled a ladder to bump against the cockpit. The pilot leapt out and down into a ring of handshaking and back-slapping.

"Ace!" the grease monkeys clamored.

"Did you get another kill?"

"How many is that now? Eight? Nine?"

"However many it is, you fellas deserve at least half the credit. When I needed some altitude, that Orkney engine sure delivered!" Ace peeled her flyer's goggles and hat off, revealing gold-flecked eyes and short-cropped gold-colored hair.

A pilot wedged in among the British and French mechanics clustered around Ace. The pilot seized Ace's hand and pumped it in both of his, muttering, "Thank you! Thank you!"

Ace was patient with it for a little while, but she disengaged and pounded the man on his leather jacket shoulder. "No big deal, Maxwell! It's why we fly in pairs. Gotta go. Time to debrief." Ace jogged off to report to the field commander.

All eyes watched her leave, becoming pensive over time.

---

[1] Biplanes built by the Société Pour L'Aviation et ses Dérivés (S.P.A.D.).

"Wot's wif you?" A British mechanic nudged the pilot.

Maxwell said thickly, "She saved my life up there."

"Ha!" barked a Frenchman, "You 'ave a debt of gratitude now, *mon ami*. 'Ow an' when will you pay it back?"

"Wot'f somethin' 'appens to 'er?" wondered the Brit.

That earned the fellow a cuff on the back of the head. *"Tais-toi!* Quiet, man! Get to working. *Tu me fatigues!"*

Ace pushed open the door.

Wing Commander Joyce Harcourt glanced up and commented drily in Oxford accents, "I thought it might be you. Market shares in breath mints rose sharply today."

"There's a career in vaudeville waiting for you after the war, Commander."

"I doubt that, Ace. Listen, congratulations. Your whole wing made it back today. The reconnaissance flight over Verviers, however, wasn't so lucky. I'm afraid Jean-Louis and Bildsten didn't return."

"They got shot down? Weren't they flying at the ceiling?"

Harcourt nodded. "Just so. Flying so high they should have been safe for at least one pass. It takes a long time for enemy planes to scramble and get up to altitude. By then, the recon planes should be halfway home."

"Bildsten. What a flyer. I can't believe they downed Bildsten."

"It isn't only Jean-Louis and Bildsten. We lost Ableton over Verviers last week."

Ace mused, "The Ottomans must have planes in the sky all the time, then. To prevent spying."

The Ottoman Empire was the enemy. The Great War began when Germany secretly joined the Empire. Almost three years of bloody conflict later, the Ottomans held Belgium, Luxembourg, and large portions of France.

Harcourt said, "Yes, and that's quite a waste of resources. There must be something deucedly important there, or the Ottomans wouldn't be protecting it like the crown jewels."

"You want me to help out, Commander?"

"Yes, I'm assigning a whole wing to Verviers reconnaissance."

"Six planes? That's almost a quarter of the Ghost Squadron![2] But the more we figure out, the quicker this war will be over," Ace replied quietly.

"Indeed. You will lead the wing."

"Me?" Ace looked evasively left and right. "But I'm just a kid."

"I know. And a girl kid at that. But you can't duck it. Not with your list of kills! It's happening already. The other pilots look to you when they need a compass bearing."

Ace stood quietly, mulling over the alien landscape

---

[2] The "Ghost Squadron" was known formally as the Royal Air Force Guest Squadron, composed of pilots and planes orphaned from other Allied military air forces, including the American Expeditionary.

of leadership.

Commander Harcourt let her stew, looking for signs of panic in the young, serious face. Seeing none, she said, "Captain—"

Ace groaned. "I've been Captain for what, three days?"

"Yes, the awful price of becoming an ace pilot. Speaking of that, how many kills today, Captain?"

"Two," Ace replied.

"Two! I'll just write that down. Dismissed." Harcourt gave a sketch of a salute.

Ace saluted back. "My machine gun jammed after the first, though."

Commander Harcourt narrowed her eyes at Ace. "How did you get a second kill without a machine gun?"

"I winked at him," Ace said, reaching for the door knob.

The tall, golden pilot left.

Looking at the closed door, Commander Harcourt muttered, "I halfway believe her!"

Ace closed the door on the noise of the officers' mess, still chewing a mouthful of stale biscuit. She fled toward the hangars.

Two mechanics were working on her SPAD. One sliced off bullet-damaged skin. The other patched with fabric and dope. When the glue-soaked fabric dried, it would be stiff and airtight, but not bulletproof. In the quiet, a sullen east wind brought muted thunder from artillery at the front.

"*Bonsoir*, Ace!"

Ace frowned. "Finished with the aileron already? Rats. I was going to help."

"So sad! You are too slow! Go find Tripod. 'E salvage some parts over there." The mechanic pointed with his knife toward the back corner of the hangar.

"Oh! Thanks!" Ace jogged over to a pool of electric light under which was the front end of a broken-backed SPAD. A wiry figure hunched over the dented radial engine. His wrench hand was missing its pinkie and ring fingers.

Tripod glanced at Ace and gestured with his head to a tool box. With a silent smile, Ace joined the disassembly. They laid out spark plugs, poppet valves, and pushrods, sorting out good parts from damaged parts.

Over a happy hour, a satisfying fatigue stole over the warm muscles of arms and shoulders. Ace took a break to stretch. She asked, "What's your name?"

"Taha Hakim Tali." Tripod's teeth gleamed white in his dark face. "Tripod is easier. I don't mind. Tap that piston. Do you think the metal is fatigued?"

Ace struck the gleaming cylinder with her wrench, listening to its ting. She nodded. "Yes. The steel is getting brittle. It's trash. Where are you from? You're the only one here with skin darker than mine."

"Algeria."

"Oh, I'm sorry. It's as rough in Algeria as it is in France."

"My town is invaded now," Tripod said. "I hope my mother and sister are all right."

"My dad's safe in America."

"You are American?"

"Indian-American. My mother was Indian, but she died when I was small. My father raised me."

"Your father is a mechanic?"

Ace laughed softly. "No, he builds ships. But he made sure I was educated." She smiled ruefully. "Well-educated. *Really* well-educated."

Tripod's eyes narrowed. "Such a scholar? Maybe you belong with the officers, not here in the grease."

"No!"

Tripod chuckled. "Why do you say no? Do the men chase you?"

"Not often."

"*Mais oui*. You have a certain look you make. A stare that is like ice water."

"What? No, I meant that I'm not good-looking."

Tripod was unconvinced. "So why do you come here, and not stay with the officers?"

"I get impatient. I can't stand being idle. I don't talk just for the sake of talking."

"Well, you belong somewhere."

Ace muttered, "Maybe. Maybe not. I do fine on my own. I've got to go. I've got to make sure they un-jammed my machine gun."

Harcourt kept the RAF[3] couriers busy. She sent in a letter recommending Cecilia "Ace" Carroway for dou-

---

[3] Royal Air Force

ble ace status, the first pilot in the Ghost Squadron to down ten planes. She also sent two letters that began "It is with heartfelt sympathy and deep regret …" for Jean-Louis's and Bildsten's next of kin. Finally, Commander Harcourt sent six pilots off to die.

Potentially, anyway. Although she maintained a properly British stoic exterior, wartime decisions made Harcourt queasy. But she knew there was something near Verviers, Belgium that the Ottomans did not want seen.

Knotted stomach or not, Harcourt scribbled the order for six planes to reconnoiter Verviers. It was a lot to throw at one recon mission, but Harcourt had a hunch it might be worth it. If the planes came back. If the planes did not come back, she would have to write more letters of condolence.

And so, shortly after dawn, six biplanes lifted into the skies over France and flew into the rising sun.

Chapter 2

Ace relaxed en route to Verviers, jawing on some double mint chewing gum. The frigid high-altitude air pinched at her nose and burrowed into a loose seam on her glove, turning her index finger into an icicle. "I love flying," Ace remarked. She sat on her hand to warm her finger up and scanned the landscape as they overflew the front lines. The bomb craters and churned turf contrasted with the colorful onset of autumn in field and forest. A few puffs of smoke erupted from Ottoman-held ground. Moments later, explosive blooms flowered in mid-air, but far below Ace's position. Ace's gum-chewing continued, tempo unaltered. "They're wasting shells. We're too high."

The gunners gave up. The wing flew over the former France-Belgium border, now many miles into Ottoman-held territory. Ace patted her instrument panel affectionately. Ace's biplane was a month old but already battered and patched from the action it had seen. Many pilots complained that the SPAD controls were sluggish and heavy, but Ace applied her analytical mind. She tested the biplane's responses until she could loop tight, roll dizzily, and pull out of vertical power dives.

Ace looked left and right. She was like the lead goose in a "V" formation. Maxwell flew on her left wing. Ace motioned the "eyes peeled" gesture and got thumbs-up yesses in return.

Maxwell saw them first: two dark dots against the bright morning sky, but well above them, not below. Maxwell stabbed his finger at the spot, and all eyes along the ragged row of aircraft were riveted on the dots. The pilots exchanged worried looks. How could planes fly so high? As the distance between the wing and the two Ottoman planes closed, it became clear. These planes were a new design. They were similar in body to the Eindecker but bigger, with two engines, not one. Two engines meant more power, and that translated to a higher altitude ceiling.

Ace furrowed her brow in worry, then motioned for her wing to spread out. They were about to be dived on and strafed, and there wasn't a thing anybody could do to prevent it.

All the airplanes stayed on the same course for an eerie minute as the distance closed. And then everything started to happen at once. The two strange Ottoman planes dived. The Allied planes dodged like drunk hummingbirds. Orange muzzle flares flashed angrily. Ace drew the fire of one, and Maxwell the other. Ace banked hard. Bullet impacts vibrated through the frame of the SPAD. She nosed into a spiraling dive, chasing where she thought the Ottoman had gone.

Ace caught a glimpse of Maxwell's plane. It coughed smoke. Its rudder flapped uselessly. All of the other four Allied planes seemed to be chasing Maxwell's attacker. Ace chased hers alone, firing a quick burst with her single gun as it lurched past her crosshairs.

Her quarry outdistanced her. Its twin motors were simply better. Much better.

Ace spiraled into a climb. She looked down to see Maxwell heading west. His engine sputtered and smoked. The other Ottoman plane also trailed smoke from its right engine with all four of her wingmates pursuing hotly. When the Ottoman's smoking engine quit altogether, the Allies would catch up and somebody was going to get a kill.

Ace eyed her adversary in the twin-Eindecker. It banked and climbed, chasing her upwards.

She dove, as a feint.

The Ottoman took the bait and pitched downwards.

Ace pulled up on the stick, hard. The SPAD had plenty of speed and arced around in a loop. Bullets from the Ottoman marked the SPAD's tail, and then it arced up and over.

Ace triggered her gun from an upside down position. Her bullets traced a ragged line down the center of the fuselage.

Ace barrel-rolled back to right-side up and chased the twin-engined Ottoman. The plane still had the speed advantage, but, oddly, it did not turn to strafe her or climb. It wove unsteadily in the air and dropped in altitude.

Ace frowned and muttered to herself, "What's going on?"

She looked around, seeing the receding dots of her wingmates but no new enemies. She looked down and blinked in surprise. Five gigantic hangars sat side by side like cozy caterpillars. Huge even for airships. The sleek, ribbed front half of an airship protruded from one hangar. It filled the vast space. "Well, that explains things!" Airships could carry huge loads of bombs and could fly much higher than any airplane.

She chased her quarry toward Verviers. Clouds shifted. Next to the five airship hangars, the outlines of an airstrip and a cluster of smaller hangars appeared. Ace muttered, "A whole airfield? I'll have a lot of company in five minutes if I stay!" She broke off the chase, banking back toward France.

Her engine coughed.

Ace gripped her controls tight. Her knuckles went ghost white.

The engine coughed again.

She rammed the choke in.

The engine seemed to purr for a while, then sputtered to a halt.

"Dry as dust," Ace groaned in the abrupt quiet. "My fuel tank must have been holed."

Ace looked around. The twin-engine Ottoman had dropped a lot of altitude. It swooped back toward the airship hangars and the accompanying airbase.

Without any push from the engine, her SPAD was a poor glider. The enemy landing strip was her only option. Ace banked toward it. Her Ottoman quarry banked unsteadily to and fro. Short of the landing strip, its gyrations ended in a dive. It plummeted straight into the ground, erupting in an inferno of burning gasoline.

Ace winced. "I must've nicked the pilot."

She could already see trucks and soldiers fanning out below her.

As a point of pride, Ace made a perfect landing.

As a matter of survival, she raised both hands high in the air as forty armed soldiers surrounded her.

Chapter 3

Commander Harcourt ripped open the letter. She read. Her brows knitted.

"Underage? Ace is sixteen?" she blurted, aghast.

Harcourt hurried to a file cabinet and riffled through folders until she found the one labeled, "Carroway, C." Her moving finger soon found the block marked "D.O.B." and she mentally subtracted.

"Gads. She lied. She said she was eighteen." Harcourt slapped the folder shut again.

She reread the letter. She slumped in her chair. "Well, there's no help for it. It'll be a dishonorable discharge. I'll have to send her home when she gets back from Verviers."

Joyce Harcourt massaged her temples and closed her eyes.

She looked up. "On the bright side, she'll make it out of this war alive."

But Ace did not return from Verviers.

Two battered men looked up as the cell door was unlocked and thrown open. A burly guard dumped a body inside.

The captives leapt to their feet. The uniformed

guard sneered at the two. "Filthy Yankee scum. You try tricks, we shoot you. Ha!" The guard slammed the door shut, then secured its heavy lock with an emphatic snick.

As soon as the guard was gone, both men knelt by the inert body in a torn flight suit.

The two men made an odd pair. One was abnormally tall, yet gangly and lean. He addressed the smaller one, who was round in face and body. "Sam? You wouldn't happen t' be a doctor, would you?"

The short, umber-skinned man replied with impeccable diction, "No, sahib. I am a cryptologist, as I told you. That is why I am here in the torture pen and not out in the slave yard."

They lifted the woman to a cot. It was not easy. The woman was tall and heavy, despite a trim frame. That she had been beaten was obvious. Dried blood stained the golden skin below her nose and on her chin. Her military insignia had been ripped from her blood-flecked flight suit.

Bruises purpled the men's visible skin. They wore stained, rumpled trousers and undershirts.

"Ah reckon she's with th' RAF," drawled the lean, tall man in soft El Paso accents.

Sam said, "Such a strong face. She might be Isis, come to earth. That is to say, under the bruises, of course. I hope she does not have broken bones along with the multiple contusions. Tombstone? I think she is coming to consciousness."

Eyes, also golden in color, focused on the men, flicking back and forth, gauging their expressions. Seeing only sympathy and concern, her rising body tension relaxed.

"The interrogators. Their mothers would be very disappointed in them!" Ace mumbled through split, swollen lips, blood sticky on her tongue.

"Please, do not do other than rest, milady," said Sam.

"B'cause there's nowhere to go if you did git up, fer one. Ah'm Tombstone, ma'am. This is Sam."

"Sam. Tombstone. A pleasure. Call me Ace. Where am I? Looks like Ace is in a hole." Ace levered herself up to scan the cell. Four cots barely fit in the spartan room. It was otherwise completely bare.

"They call it Camp 68, milady," said Sam.

"Ah think we're in Germany, but still west o' th' Rhine. That's a guess. It ain't like they've drawn us any pictures or nuthin'," said Tombstone.

"They questioned me," Ace said euphemistically.

Sam said, "Yes, Lady Ace. You appear to be a pilot. You would be interrogated, of course. I am so very, very sorry."

"Sam's a cryptologist, Ace, ma'am, so they're always trying to get him to crack codes. I know a thing or two 'bout electricity, but I think they're realizin' I ain't got no secrets to tell 'em."

Distant, muted shouting of orders leaked through the solid walls of the cell. A rushed march of booted feet. Sounds of trucks cranking to life and roaring away.

The lock of the cell door rattled. Ace struggled to her feet. Herds of horses galloped around the inside of her skull. Tombstone and Sam balled their fists up, but defiance was useless. Six guards with batons and shackles swarmed in. Chained in short order, the trio found themselves on a forced march.

The guards spoke in German as they roughly yanked their prisoners outside into wan sunlight. The words "Darko Dor" were repeated a few times.

The Ottomans stuffed Ace, Sam, and Tombstone into the back of a covered truck. Their shackles were fastened to U-bolts in the truck bed. They joined three other prisoners already chained in place.

A very broad, pale-skinned man with red hair, a two-week beard, and bulging muscles looked at them with one eye. His other eye was blackened and swollen shut. He remarked in thick Cockney accents words not known by most London East-enders, "We're perambulating into terra incognita!"

Tombstone groaned. "Oh, who invited you, Gooper? Ding-nab it! Out o' th' fryin' pan and into th' fire! I ain't sure I kin stand bein' cooped up with this here blubbery Brit!"

"Tombstone? Blimey! Eject the underweight debauchee!" retorted Gooper.

Dark Sam was very short and round in shape. Leathery Tombstone was tall and lean as a rake. Pale Gooper was as broad as he was tall, with hulking shoulders and arms and no neck at all. The remaining two men were of average proportions, also battered and ragged. The dark-haired one pointed to the blond one accusingly. He spoke in a broad Boston accent. "Ditto for me! Of all the bum luck! I'm still stuck with you, Quack!"

"Stuff it, Brat," replied the blond man nicknamed Quack. His voice was melodious and deep.

"Bert! It's short for Hubert."

"Stuff it, Brat," persisted Quack.

Bert flushed around his bruises.

Truck doors slammed. The engine turned over and rattled to life, and the truck lurched off.

Ace was still. All five men were older than she. More experienced. Their banter spoke of fiery, unbroken spirits. Ace meditated on the value of five undaunted souls, chained in body. Vistas of possibility made her eyes sparkle with new light. Ace took a deep breath, painful due to bruised ribs. A memory surfaced.

"Arabic!" commanded Fitzhugh Royston, Ph.D., GBE.

"Tushariq alshams fi alsabah," piped Cecilia Carroway, staring fixedly at her tutor's waistcoat buttons, which were at eye level.

"German!"

"Die Sonne geht morgens auf."

"Swedish!"

"Solen stiger på morgonen."

"I don't believe you," said the towering tutor.

Little Cecilia hesitated. "I think I said it correctly, Sir Fitzhugh,."

"Even the most trivial of phrases, child, should be delivered with utmost conviction. Else, why say it?"

Cecilia stayed quiet.

The silence stretched.

Sir Fitzhugh, spoke warmly. "Excellent. You learn. Now, in English, and like you mean it."

"The sun rises in the morning!"

"Yes. Yes, it does. Quite so."

Ace spoke as if she meant it. "Introductions are in order. I'm Ace Carroway. That's Sam and that's Tombstone. I take it you three are Gooper, Quack, and Bert?"

"Aye, Gooper. Oim a British Regular."

"Quack will do, ma'am. Field medic."

"I'm Bert, American Expeditionary."

The truck hit a pothole and gave a jarring bounce.

"Ow! My bruises are getting bruised," Quack said.

Sam said, "Does anyone know where we are going?"

Ace's vistas of possibility sharpened. She sucked in another breath for courage, then made the leap of optimism. "We are going to an experimental airplane facility near St. Vith, Belgium, on the orders of Ottoman Minister for Technology Darko Dor. They pulled six prisoners they thought might be capable of skilled technical labor. We are to help them build airplanes."

Five pairs of round eyes (really four-and-a-half pairs, given Gooper's black, swollen orb) goggled at the bloodied young woman. She sat outwardly composed, steady golden eyes meeting theirs.

"How did you know all that, Lady Ace?" queried Sam.

"I speak German. Our guards were talkative. As for Darko Dor, his name's in the newspapers, though maybe not on the front page. He's in charge of airplane factories, among other things."

"Ace. Is that more than just a nickname?" queried Bert.

Tombstone answered, "She ain't said, but I betcha she's a bona fide flying ace."

"Just 'Ace' will do." She grinned as far as her swollen lips would allow.

Despite twinges from her ribs, she stuck out her hand. One by one, the men shook, solemn and firm. The handshakes felt right.

The truck stopped at a checkpoint. Three gun-toting guards joined them in the back, stopping further conversation.

The truck rattled and bounced onward over war-torn roads, heading for St. Vith.

CHAPTER 4

The *Flugzeugfabrik*[4] at St. Vith had been a private airstrip before the Great War, little more than a runway and a shed. After the Ottomans overwhelmed Belgium, Darko Dor issued orders for a new hangar, workroom, and barracks. The old barn and farmhouse remained. The airstrip was lengthened and hastily paved. The terrain consisted of cultivated valleys poking between forested mountain ridges. Forest enclosed the facility on three sides, beyond the chain-link fence.

Three new guards accompanied the new prisoners. At first, the prisoners dug out a pit for a new latrine. Before day's end, they built the latrine itself.

The massive, red-haired Gooper smashed a nail with a hammer. The nail popped into place meekly. Gooper announced, "Oi! Done! That's that. Fastidious as a royal nanny."

"Put down the hammer. Follow me!" the guard with the birthmark over his eye instructed in broken English. His rifle was always in his hands, as if it was permanently attached.

For a brief moment, Gooper did not obey. He hefted the hammer in his right hand and sized up the guard, giving every impression that he liked the odds. The guard raised his rifle. Gooper tossed the hammer nonchalantly aside and lumbered after the guard. "Par-

---

[4] Airplane factory.

don, guv'nor! It's yer accent. Blinkin' 'ard ter understand yeh!"

"*Who's* hard to understand now?" teased Tombstone, who was oiling the latrine door hinges.

"Silence! Follow me!" The surly guard gestured
with the business end of his rifle.

The guard herded the five men and Ace across the
yard into the workroom. The workroom was a large
shed full of saws, grinders, presses, forges, hand tools,
and stacks of airplane parts. The air smelled of grease,
flame, and ozone. "Get in a line! Inspection!"

The six Allies made a line in leisurely fashion, push-
ing the edge of disobedience. They made an odd sight.
Tall, gawky Tombstone, short, distinguished Sam,
bulky Gooper, and average Bert and Quack, clustered
around a quiet woman with alert eyes and regal pos-
ture. Twenty people in mechanic's coveralls, mostly
men, gathered opposite them.

From an office in the corner four more men came.
One wore a business suit, and two wore Ottoman military uniforms with officer bars. The fourth man's uniform was a blank dark gray. Shiny new boots clicked
when he walked. He had slicked-back black hair and a
tiny, fashionable goatee. His lips curled in a permanent
sneer that marred an otherwise pleasant face. He did
all the talking.

"Good day to you," he addressed the crowd of mechanics in a Slavic accent, placing his hands behind his
back. "I have good news. The *Falke* has been ap-
proved for mass production. We will continue to make
them here. Furthermore, production will be duplicated
in Antwerp. Congratulations."

Obediently, the mass of mechanics clapped their

hands in applause. The row of Allies kept stoic.

The man with the blank uniform continued, "Twelve of you are new to the *Flugzeugfabrik*. Congratulations on your promotion. I know you will serve the Emperor well." He gestured to the row of prisoners. "To speed up production, these prisoners will assist. The claim is that they have some skill." He sneered with distaste as he looked at the Allies. He glanced to the officer at his left. "Get them cleaned up! They look like rats! Put armbands on their coveralls to mark them as prisoners."

The officer clicked his heels. "*Jawohl*, Minister Dor!"

Darko Dor told the flock of airplane-builders, "These prisoners will be watched. They will work hard. If they do not, report them, and it will be," he glanced at the prisoners with a smirk, "taken care of."

He sauntered toward the prisoners, looking them up and down as if they were cattle at auction and he was considering placing a bid. None of the prisoners made any overt signs of rebellion, but none of them did any cringing, either. In silky tones Darko Dor lectured the Allies, "You will have no second chances. If you are unskilled, you go back to Camp 68. If you *try* anything, you will have no need to travel. Your dead body will be buried here."

He turned to the mechanics again. "They are yours to order about. We can get more prisoners if it helps with production. Your orders: increase production on the *Falke*! Ten planes per week!" The Minister of Technology sketched a minimal salute. "Dismissed!"

Darko Dor's eyes lingered on Ace before he snapped around and disappeared into the office, followed by an officer.

The man in the suit paced and consulted a clip-board. He nibbled at the end of a pencil.

The officer that was told to find work clothes for the prisoners looked at them blankly for a minute. Finally, he turned to a nearby worker starting to operate a drill press. "Get them clothes!" He pivoted to the guards. "Bring them back here when they are dressed!" He strutted out the main door, work done. He angled toward the farmhouse, now the officers' quarters and kitchen.

CHAPTER 5

The guard with the birthmark over his eye herded the prisoners back to their makeshift prison in the barn. Their cell was not yet built. Instead, a large iron spike was driven into the ground. Six chains radiated from it, ending in ankle irons.

The guard shackled Tombstone and Sam. Bert looked at the bare earth of the barn floor and quipped, "Do I detect mud on my divan? Inform the staff immediately."

The guard turned on Bert with teeth bared. "I speak English, you American pig! You are a prisoner! You have no rights!"

Bert was sullen. "Says who?"

"My name is Uwe. But you are to call me 'sir'." The guard named Uwe spat into Bert's face. "Piggy scum!"

Bert's fists clenched. He threw a roundhouse right hook that clipped Uwe along the cheekbone.

Ace's eyes flew wide and she inhaled, a memory flooding into her mind.

"We are in the market today to learn about surprise," Master Jitsuko said, her voice peaceful as always. "It is getting hard to surprise you in the dojo."

The gawky Cecilia towered over the compact Wing Chun master as they threaded through market stalls. As they neared the Osaka waterfront, more and more stalls sold fish. Jitsuko's warning on surprise was plenty to put Cecilia on edge. When she sensed a whir in the air, she was ready. She spun, jabbing fist properly tucked back, then slamming forward and up … right into a halibut. There was a wet splat and a petite spray of fish mucus.

"Ew!" Cecilia blurted, shocked. She stared at the fishmonger who had tried to clobber her. He smiled, but raised the halibut to attempt to slap her again. Several other fishermen jumped in, attempting to beat the gangly girl to the ground.

Cecilia did not emerge unslimed, but neither did she get smacked to the pavement. Later, Jitsuko gave what Cecilia interpreted as praise. "Next time, no hint for you!"

Sam and Tombstone could do nothing but rattle their chains, but Gooper and Quack charged Uwe. Gooper got a hand on Uwe's rifle and Quack dove for Uwe's midsection.

Ace moved with the swiftness of a striking cobra. Within the span of a heartbeat there were three meaty thwacks.

Gooper grunted, "Mff!"

Quack squawked, "Gah!"

Bert outgassed, "Uff!"

All three hit the dirt.

Ace rose from her fighting crouch, calmly saying to Uwe, "Shackle us. We will not resist." She looked pointedly at the five male prisoners.

Uwe moved to obey Ace immediately. Under Ace's formidable gaze, all remained silent and cooperative. Uwe clicked the shackles shut.

Ace continued to Uwe, "Now go put some ice on that cheek. Go on."

Uwe made a motion as if saluting Ace, but he checked it. He turned in flustered silence and walked out of the barn, rubbing his cheek.

Ace clasped her hands behind her back. When Uwe was out of sight, she said softly, "Sorry about that, Bert. Gooper. Quack."

Gooper was shaking his red-haired head back and forth, and rubbing a bruised solar plexus. "Ace. Yer part 'uman, part *Ovis canadensis.*"

Tombstone narrowed his eyes at Gooper. "Stop makin' words up, ya throwback."

"He means bighorn sheep, Tombstone. The ones with big, curly horns that charge each other and collide at full tilt." Ace smiled lopsidedly. "I'll take it as a compliment. Also, I want to talk about delaying our escape."

"Eh? You're not going to call me out on being a hothead?" Bert was contrite.

"No, Bert. I wanted to punch him too. He's a little weasel." Ace's voice dropped low and her eyes defocused. "But I think we should be strategic. We have bigger game than weasels to hunt. We can't do that if we rebel too soon."

Sam asked, "What did you mean, just now, Lady Ace? Your words were '*delaying* escape.'"

"I mean that I want to do some sabotage before escaping. Why escape with a whisper when you can escape with a bang?" Ace wore a wry smile.

"Ohhhh!" Quack said.

Ace held up a hand. "I want it unanimous. If anybody wants to make a run for the front lines immediately, then that's the way it will be. We'll escape at the earliest opportunity."

Gooper put his hands behind his neck as if lounging, bulging biceps in full display. "Conservatism? Bah!

Can't abide the stuff."

Tombstone drawled, "Ah ain't in no hurry."

Quack chuckled. "How do you say *saboteur* in German?"

Bert snorted. "You pronounce it 'saboteur,' you hack. But right now that word is music to my ears. Ten aircraft a week, that goatee'd Ottoman said. It's food for thought."

Everyone looked at Sam. Sam was the smallest in stature. Judging by appearances, he far more resembled a mouse than a lion. But, smiling beatifically, teeth gleaming white in his sepia face, he said, "I vote sabotage."

Ace nodded solemnly, as if a pact had been sealed. "Thanks, fellas! So we'll play it cool. We won't make waves. They are serious about shooting prisoners. They probably *want* to shoot one of us, to instill terror in the rest of us. Let's not give them a chance. Let's look like good workers while we learn as much as we can. Then sabotage. Then escape. Agreed?"

There was a chorus of affirmatives.

A dubious mechanic arrived, six white coveralls in his arms.

Chapter 6

A week crawled by. The guard named Uwe took to persecuting Bert. Perhaps Bert's left hook was unforgivable, or perhaps Bert's Beacon Hill mannerisms triggered buried loathings in the guard's soul. Whatever the reason, Uwe was not content to let a day go by without humiliating or, better yet, injuring Bert.

The airplane assembly work provided a break from the abuse. Most of the Allies drilled, buffed, tapped, riveted, and fastened in the noisy workroom. But Sam's affinity for power tools was lackluster. He found a niche in the office, keeping track of parts inventories. The Allied prisoners found acceptance and even welcome among the factory workers. Half the mechanics were conscripted from other places around the Empire. These worked unwillingly, dreaming of escape to their homelands.

Ace was in a category by herself. The officers wanted her stationed near to them in the capacity of housecleaner or cook. But orders were orders. Ace was assigned to airplane assembly. Ace stationed herself in the final assembly hangar without asking permission. No one objected. No one was quite sure what to make of the tall, silent young woman, but she knew how to handle a wrench.

Ace discovered that the *"Falke[5]"* was exactly the

---

[5] Falcon.

twin-engine fighter that she had managed to shoot down over Verviers. On a normal plane, the engine sat ahead of the pilot. On the twin-engine *Falke*, the engines were on the wings. That meant extra complexity so the pilot could control both throttles and both chokes via cables and levers. Ace studied the *Falke* down to each rivet, as thoroughly as her childhood lessons. By week's end, she was giving pointers to the Ottoman mechanics, not the other way around.

In addition to airplane assembly, the prisoners had to finish construction on their own cell. They nailed and bolted thick timbers in a shell around the latrine. The barn-jail was chilly by day, but bitter cold by night. In the mornings, teeth chattered and fingers moved stiffly.

Tombstone's large feet were half frozen each morning. His boots had once been hobnail trench boots, but the Ottomans had ripped out all the metal studs. Now, the soles looked like Swiss cheese, and Tombstone had to rub and chafe his feet back to life each morning before he could walk on them.

On day three, the shackles came off and the prisoners slept on cots in their cell rather than on the dirt floor.

"Oi almost feel loike an *'omo sapiens* again!" Gooper cooed, relaxing on a cot for the first time, his muscled arms folded behind his head.

"Funny, you don't *look* much like one o' them," Tombstone prodded.

"Better *Homo erectus* than *Homo lacerta*." Gooper stuck out his tongue at Tombstone.

Tombstone frowned. "All right. I give up. What's *lacerta* in English?"

"Lizard, you lizard man." Gooper batted his eyelashes.

The next morning, Ace exercised. As she warmed up with stretches, she clenched her jaw resolutely. Her defiant eyes mutely challenged any of her fellow prisoners to comment. None of the gentlemen did. To a man, they worked hard to avert their eyes. Recognizable calisthenics segued into gymnastic exercises requiring strength and flexibility. Gooper happened to look over at a moment when Ace was inverted, feet straining toward the sky, her entire weight supported by the splayed fingertips of one hand. "Blimey! I hain't never seen the like!" After gymnastics, Ace settled into a meditative pose. Although her eyes were closed, she perspired as if expending even greater effort than before. The men found that glancing at Ace during this stage triggered an uncomfortable empathy, after which they found themselves mopping their own sweating foreheads. Finally, in a rapid-fire whisper, Ace recited multiplication tables that extended into the millions.

The men soon learned that it was a daily ritual, carried over from Ace's childhood. The routine was never exactly the same. Some days, instead of multiplication tables, it was logarithms. Once, she asked for ancient calendar dates. One of the men would invent a year, month, and day, and she would reply with the day of the week. None of the males doubted that she was correct, though none of them could prove it.

After their four cell walls shut out the guards, it was sometimes possible to talk amongst themselves.

"Tell us about yourself, Sam," suggested an alto voice one night. "Start with your name."

"Lady Ace, I do not think it very important, but I

will say. I am named Sam Raia Biming. My father is Chinese. My mother is Egyptian."

"Sam is your real name? It's not a nickname? What a disappointment!" said Bert.

"Go on, Sam," Ace said.

"Yes. I was educated in Beijing and Cairo. I apprenticed at the British Museum of London in the field of archaeology. Egyptology was my first passion, but I branched out from there into prehistory and also cultural anthropology and geology. The war came. An officer in the museum heard me speak of Egyptian hieroglyphs. A few days later, I was invited to the department of intelligence, code breaking division, to see if I would be of use. I saw no action, unlike the other brave and admirable members of this party."

"How'd ya end up captured?" Tombstone asked.

"My coming to be a prisoner was an accident. I was being sent to a radio transmitter near Lyon, France by plane. My plane went off course."

"Well, you've seen action now, mate!" chortled Gooper.

"What about you, Gooper?"

Gooper did not answer. Ace encouraged, "Go on. Please?"

"Ow … Awright. Me name's Phileas Locknard. Born an' raised in East London."

"Before the war, what were you doing?"

"College. First Locknard at uni, they say. Biology."

"Biology?"

"Yeh! Love it! When I was small, me mum took me to a park. She could 'ardly get me ter leave. I was strokin' the grass and watchin' bugs crawl. I 'ave loved biological science ever since. That, an' rugby."

"How did you end up in a POW camp?"

"When war broke out, I signed up, like every other bloke did. If the Emperor in Istanbul wants Brits to bow to 'im, 'e's got a long, long pass to pull off. In the Regulars, I learned ter shoot an' drive. I fought at Rouen, Beauvais, an' Soissons. But we lost that 'un. I was knocked out an' woke up a prisoner."

Tombstone said, "Thereby inflictin' his red-haired, blobby self on us!"

"Ow, put a sock in it, cowpoke. I could tie yew in a knot, bone boy."

"You jes' try it, ya ginger donkey butt."

"Shh!" Ace hissed. The barn door rolled back. Footsteps of guards crunched outside the wooden-walled cell.

Chapter 7

During her daily exercise regimen, while standing on her head, Ace was amused to discover that a series of planks on the outer wall, the wall that separated them from the outside, had been neatly sawed almost through, so that a series of swift kicks would open a passage to freedom, big enough even for Gooper to scoot through. The cuts were hidden by a strip of wooden trim, lightly tacked into place.

"Who made these escape cuts?" Ace inquired that night, voice pitched in a whisper, mindful of a guard stationed somewhere outside. "Wait, let me guess! Hmm. Sam probably thought of it, and I bet Gooper served as an obstacle to block the line of sight. Bert and Quack were too busy arguing, so it must have been Tombstone."

"Right th' first time, Miz Ace!" said Tombstone.

Sam said, "Lady Ace, are you sure you wish to wait to try to escape?"

"Definitely. Darko Dor has left, as you know. He'll return with a truckload of brand new engines from Frankfurt next week. We'll escape a few days after that. Keep in mind we'll have to trek a few days through the woods. We'll be hunted."

"Why wait for th' engines?" rumbled Gooper.

"Shhh!" scolded Tombstone, urging Gooper to quiet.

"We'll rig them to fail. It will probably work out

that I will do this, since I have been assigned to the hangar." Ace's phraseology was misleading. Hangar-work had been her idea from the start.

"Ohhh!" Gooper said as understanding dawned. He added, aside to Tombstone, "Ow, *you* shush! Colonial hick!"

"Bloated ginger lowbrow!"

"Coriaceous saurian!" Gooper's capacious supply of big words always sounded particularly alien when spoken in his broad Cockney accent.

"Ruhe! [6]" barked the guard outside, punctuating his shout of "quiet!" by pounding the butt of his rifle on the locked door.

On day eight, there was a brief surge of panic amongst the guards and officers. Ace was referred to as *die Alibifrau[7]* among the guards and officers, even though there were other women among the airplane workers. On this occasion, *die Alibifrau* was nowhere to be seen.

Sam noticed the subtle yet electric air of frantic searching. An officer hurried into the workhouse office where Sam was filing paperwork. There was a brief, hushed discussion with the business-suited manager. Sam caught the emotional timbre and the words *"die Alibifrau."* The next minute, the men both left, and

---

[6] Quiet!

[7] The woman.

Sam sauntered out after them unnoticed. The manager left for the hangar. The officer lingered outside the workhouse and scanned around, turning in place to view the airstrip and buildings, and the fields and forest beyond. There was a tall chain-link fence around the whole facility with curls of barbed wire festooning the top.

Sam boldly stepped out too, and asked in casual, solicitous tones, "Sir. May I help you find something?"

The irritated officer frowned at Sam. After a short moment of indecision, the officer said, "*Ja!* The woman. Have you seen her?"

Sam looked toward the hangar, seeing a pair of guards searching with growing urgency. They peeked behind obstacles and buildings, trotting in their haste. Sam glanced toward the farmhouse. Ace casually stepped from the house's front door into plain sight. Sam smoothly told the officer in sympathetic tones, while nodding his head wisely, "Why, yes, sir. She went into the house for what I believe is called washing up, sir. She is now finished. See?" Sam gestured theatrically toward the quiet, tall woman striding toward them.

"*Verdammt Nochmal!* [8]" cursed the officer in relief. He jogged to meet Ace, then stabbed a finger toward the hangar. He was trying to look fierce, Sam could tell. Ace strode by him silently, the very picture of righteous dignity. Sam fell into step beside her.

As they approached the hangar, Sam said in a whisper, "Lady Ace. What are you up to?"

"Something not very nice. I feel positively slimy about it. But this is war, I suppose. I'll tell you all

---

[8] Bloody hell!

about it soon."

They reached the hangar. Ace went back to work. The officers and guards decided to pretend that nothing had happened. However, Ace got double-watched for the rest of the day.

That night, in the jail cell, the guards brought them bread, jerky, and water, their usual meal. Bert reached for the water, but Ace touched his arm and shook her head. It was enough. No one touched the water pitcher. When the guard wasn't looking, Ace carefully poured it out into the corner of the cell. The water disappeared into the dirt.

Later, when they were all locked in and supposedly sleeping, Bert inquired, "So. What gives with the water trick?"

Sam said, "Yes, Lady Ace. What?"

There was a guilty silence, then Ace said, "I believe *Giardia lamblia* takes a week to ten days to develop full symptoms."

Tombstone inquired, "What, now?"

Gooper chuckled, then expounded glibly, "*Giardia lamblia*. A microscopic organism. A flagellate. 'E lives almost worldwide, commonly in the intestinal tracts of deer and other woodland animals. Th' animals aren't bothered by 'im, but th' humans are! In about a week, if Ace 'as done wot I think she's done, every Jerry wot drank water tonight's gonna need the loo every ten minutes!"

Tombstone spoke in tones of wonder. "Well, rope my ankles and call me a dogie! Somebody did a brain transplant on Gooper!"

"Aw, shaddap, cowboy!" said Gooper.

"Don't you two get going!" Quack said, then asked,

"Ace? What *did* you do? I'm still lost."

Ace was quiet for a moment, then sighed. "I snuck out to the fence perimeter and snagged a deer pellet. I mixed it into the big water jug they use in the kitchen. A week from now, the whole camp will be pretty miserable, except hopefully us." She sighed again. "I feel dirty."

"Do not forget, Lady Ace, they have spilled your blood in the interrogation room. This is nothing in comparison," Sam said in his precisely enunciated, polite style.

"Hear, hear!" chimed in Bert. The spiteful guard Uwe had given Bert a painful knock on the elbow earlier in the day, and Bert was rubbing it.

A voice that sounded exactly like that of Darko Dor said, "If you *try* anything, you will have no need to travel. Your dead body will be buried here." The Slavic accents and other idiosyncrasies were perfect.

"Jiminy!" Tombstone said with amazement, "Was that you, Quack?"

Bert said, "Yah, that's him. I think he has a bright future in radio."

Quack said, in his normal rolling basso, "Radio? And deprive the stage of a talent such as mine?"

"You're too ugly. Wicked ugly."

"Envy, Bert? Tsk. It does not become you, old chum," Quack said.

Gooper said, "Them blokes are bein' obtuse 'bout it, but they're tryin' ter cheer you on, Ace. Dive inter the ruck and slug it out!"

"You fellas are the best," Ace said quietly. "If there's an 'after' to this war, we'll have a reunion and laugh about the good ol' days at the *Flugzeugfabrik*."

CHAPTER 8

Two days later, a convoy arrived. Two flatbed trucks carried new engines. A third truck hauled a load of wheels and propellers. A gleaming black car with Ottoman insignia followed shortly after.

Inside the workroom, Bert bent metal struts and Quack sewed leather upholstery. They looked up to see Minister of Technology Darko Dor sweep in. He delivered a few orders, then left as abruptly as he came. The obsequious manager bobbed his head in nervous subservience. The moment Darko Dor left, he ordered workers to unload the trucks, including Bert.

Bert went outside to wrap chains around engines. Ace ran the lifting crane. The truck driver and a guard lounged, watching the prisoners work, lazily smoking cigarettes. Uwe came to take his guard shift. He smoked his own cigarette and pointed and laughed at Bert.

Ace watched Bert flush. She frowned. One by one, Bert wrapped chains around massive engines atop the truck. Ace swung them over and down into the hangar with the powered crane. Bert hustled down from the truck to guide the engine into place on the hangar floor.

Slyly, it happened. On Bert's way down, Uwe tripped him. Bert tumbled to the tarmac, scraping the heel of his hand and bashing his forehead. He groaned and rolled to his feet. He clenched his fists and oriented on Uwe with murderous intent. But Uwe trained his rifle between Bert's eyes.

"Be careful, stupid Yankee. You wouldn't want to get yourself executed," Uwe gleefully sneered.

With great effort, Bert heaved his body away from Uwe and over to guide the engine into place. Uwe laughed and went back to joke and smoke with the driver.

"I can't take it much longer, Ace!" Bert whispered when the crane revved down.

"You can. You can take it another few days. I'm sorry, Bert."

Darko Dor sent for *die Alibifrau*. An Ottoman officer ushered Ace into the farmhouse. The gray-clad Minister of Technology was in the living room. He bowed a few inches at the waist. The escorting officer continued through the living room and into the kitchen. As he left, the officer shot a look of envy and fear toward the back of Darko's head.

At a small table, Darko had set out a bottle of wine and two glasses. Ace felt a crawling sensation in her gut as the trim, goateed man smiled and gestured to a chair. "Please. Sit."

Ace sat. In slow motion.

Darko Dor poured wine and chatted one-sidedly. "I have inquired about you. You were a pilot. You brought down a *Falke* with only a SPAD. Congratulations, Miss Carroway."

Ace sat rigid and straight-backed. Her golden skin and short hair contrasted with the white of her grease-smeared coveralls. She said no word.

"Nothing to say? Well, perhaps try the wine. It is delicious. It is only a light wine, a Reisling, nothing heavy. A small token of my esteem. My respect for such an accomplished young woman. It is not poisoned, see?" Darko took a long sip, perching on the seat opposite Ace. "I want to help you, you understand. I want to get you out of the—" he pursed his lips in distaste, "the hovel you are forced to stay in. You are used to much finer accommodations, I think."

Ace pinched the bridge of her nose where it met her forehead, as if trying to calm a headache. Her voice sounded full of suffering. "If there is a point, please get to it."

"I think you get the point already, Miss Carroway. I can take you away from all this. Find you employment. See to your needs. Ease all those burdens you carry." Darko's voice was sympathetic and soft.

He reached a soothing hand to stroke her shoulder.

Ace seemed to hear Jitsuko's voice in her ear.

"Wing Chun brings inner peace. Why?"

"It unites body and mind," Cecilia guessed.

"Yes, all right. But also it is the knowledge of personal power. Knowledge. This I can do. That is an inch too far. The ability to judge."

"Personal power. I am swift. I am strong."

"You are swift. You are strong. And now that you know it, you need never mention it again."

Darko Dor's reaching hand did not arrive. Ace stood up tall, very suddenly. The chair she had been sitting in bounced off her straightened knees and skidded backwards across the floor. "I'm not interested," she said flatly.

She about-faced and stalked out.

Darko Dor sipped wine for a full minute before remarking to the empty room, "Minds change."

No one questioned Ace when she took a chest-braced hand drill and a slender drill bit, and bored a hole in an engine block. The workers assumed that she was following orders. Sam added a requisition for two dozen more drill bits to replace those dulled by Ace's clandestine industry, and that went unnoticed too. Tombstone squirreled away a duffel bag for electrical gear stolen from the workroom. He kept it buried under the dirt floor of the cell and added to it every day. Quack took a wire cutter and hid it in his coveralls, to cut through the chain-link fence when they escaped. Bert had enough to do just to keep from exploding in the direction of the abusive Uwe.

Darko Dor's official black car vanished.

Some of the officers and guards began to feel ill.

That evening, Tombstone had a sparkle in his eye. As the guards locked them in for the evening, Tombstone displayed a stolen battery and a pair of diodes. He set to work wiring components together.

Ace watched over his shoulder. "You're a radio engineer?"

The lanky, cadaverous man replied, "Yes, ma'am.

Went t' school in electrical engineering at Austin. Didn't finish, though. The war broke out."

"What's your full name, Tombstone?"

"Gregory Jamison. I was born outside El Paso. I guess that's why I picked up the handle Tombstone when I joined the Expeditionary. They made me a sharpshooter. Shootin' comes natural. I did a lot o' shootin' as a kid."

"How did you come to be captured?"

"I was put in Gooper's unit at Soissons. Somehow, I didn't hear the retreat signal. I got surrounded an' I jes' put my hands up."

"Very sensible of you."

"You almost done with th' sabotage, Ace?"

"Almost. One more day. There are 32 new engines. I got to twenty of them so far."

"What're you up to, 'xactly?"

"I never said. There hasn't been much opportunity for talk. I drill a hole where the fuel line runs by the engine. And then I backfill the hole with solder. I polish it up bright and bolt the fuel line back into place. The hole is all but invisible, even before the fuel line gets connected."

"So ya make a hole, then fill it back up again? Whaffer?"

"The solder is soft compared with the engine block. As the engine runs, the heat will erode the solder plug away. Eventually, the solder will vaporize completely and a little flame jet will shoot out — right at the fuel line."

"Blimey!" Gooper said appreciatively.

Ace mused, "I predict the *Falke* will soon gain a reputation for being a deathtrap to fly."

"Brava!" said Bert through a lip freshly split by Uwe.

"Fire falcon. It's a catchy phrase, but I wouldn't want to pilot one," Ace said.

"Who taught you about machines, Lady Ace?" Sam asked. To him, all of this was magic.

Ace hesitated, then smiled wistfully. "My father."

"Who is your father, Lady Ace? And your mother? And may I ask your name?"

Ace laughed softly. "We're prisoners. Such details are nonessential. I'm Cecilia Carroway, daughter of Grant Carroway and Amiti Rishi."

Gooper said, "Wot? The actress? I wrote a paper on 'er in school. Siren of the Silent Screen, I called it."

"Yes, but she died when I was very young. My father raised me. I had tutors besides regular schooling. I attended university early. When the war broke out, I signed up as a pilot. I was captured when a *Falke* shot a hole in the fuel line of my SPAD."

Quack emitted a long, low whistle. "Wait! I heard about you! You were on track to be the youngest M.D. in Harvard history! It only clicked just now."

"Let's hope it qualifies me to *doctor up* this place's *Falke* production," Ace said, wiggling her eyebrows.

Bert asked, "How old are you, Ace?"

Ace fell silent.

"Oh," Bert said softly. "Can't say, eh? Well. Moving on, then."

There was some uncomfortable squirming.

Ace said testily, "If you gentlemen get any ideas of becoming *overprotective* or something, I'll … well, you

---

[9] Italian is gender sensitive. "Bravo" is male, "Brava" is female.

better not, that's all!"

"Don' get a burr under yer saddle, Ace!" Tombstone soothed. "You're a cyclone an' ain't none of us Pecos Bill enough to lasso you!"

The last day dragged on endlessly for the five men, but Ace was busy. She burned through drill bits steadily. When the manager happened by, she had a lie ready. "Installing thermometers." Since Ace was also keeping up with her regular assembly chores, the manager had no cause to fret. He went off to scold a worker that had taken a moment to wipe sweat from his brow.

Bert caught a break. Uwe was feeling queasy. He was not feeling perky enough to properly torment Bert. The guards and officers were not in view very much. They were competing with the mechanics for access to the outhouses.

At long last, the evening of escape arrived.

So did Darko Dor, along with what appeared to be a bodyguard. A heavy brute built almost as massive as Gooper, and festooned with weaponry like ornaments on a Yule tree. Darko Dor had his usual riding crop and pistol.

Supper was late, but eventually a pale green Uwe thrust bread and water at the prisoners. The newly-arrived bodyguard loomed behind him.

And then came a sudden, unforeseen complication.

Uwe stabbed a finger at Ace and said, "You. Woman. You come to the house."

Ace stirred to obey, but before she left the cell, she mumbled a string of apparent gibberish. Sam's eyes widened.

The bulky bodyguard escorted Ace off, one of his many guns prodding her between the shoulder blades.

CHAPTER 9

The tense men did not feel like eating, but wolfed down the bread anyway so that Uwe would go away. After an interminable time, he did. He sneered at them, locked the cell door, and crunched away over the gravel.

"What do we do now?" groaned blond Quack.

"What are they doing with Ace?" Bert wanted to know.

"Gentlemen," said Sam.

"I say we bust up the whole place!" Gooper smacked a ham fist into a meaty palm.

"Aww, keep your hat on. You're not bulletproof, you knuckleheaded Limey," said Tombstone.

"Gentlemen," said Sam.

"Sam, you're not helping. We're trying to figure out what to do," Quack said.

Bert said, "We could bust out, even get past the fence. But that would leave Ace still caught here!"

Suddenly, two fleshy slaps rang out. Gooper and Quack, who were nearest to Sam, rocked sideways, grunted in pain, then stared at Sam in amazement. Sam glared back, fists balled up. He had walloped them both on the jaw so fast they didn't see the blows coming.

"Sahibs. What I am trying to say to you is that Ace left instructions. And now, you need to be quiet and listen to me."

"Pardner, I ain't never seen you more emphatic. Boys, let's give Sam a listen," Tombstone said, a distinct note of appreciation in his voice.

"Thank you, Tombstone. Now, the country of my origin is Egypt. Ace knew this, and also she knows enough of the Egyptian language to have given me instructions as she was led away."

"Care to tell us what she said?" Quack mumbled, rubbing his aching jaw.

"She told us that we should escape as soon as the coast is clear, and she will catch up to us." Sam paused to rub his own knuckles. "The coast is clear. We should go."

Tombstone immediately started digging in the floor. That was where he had left his collection of stolen tools. He said, "Awlright, Sam, but ... one more li'l thing. Do you think Ace would mind if the fuel depot kinda, uh, blew up?"

"Good heavens, what a question!" Bert said. He also jumped into action, tearing off the bit of molding that hid their saw marks. He used the heel of his hand to remove the planks as quietly as possible. If any guards had been near, they would have heard the splintering sounds. But they were not. They were in the outhouses.

"I am sure she would not object, Tombstone," Sam said.

Quack grabbed his stolen wire cutters. He was the first one through the hole.

"Blow up the fuel? How d'ye think you're going ter manage that, you barmy stick?" Gooper said. "The fuel depot's 'alfway across the field, an' in the opposite direction we're going in!"

They scrambled out through the hole in the barn wall and beelined for the perimeter fence. They nervously glanced over their shoulders. But the night was moonless, and the grounds were not lit with electric lights the way a prison would be. There was no sign any alarm had been raised.

They piled up behind the chain-link fence. The top of the fence was looped with razor wire. They all preferred that Quack cut them a hole rather than getting lacerated climbing over the top. Past the fence lay fifty yards of sloping field, and beyond that the forested flank of a mountain.

Tombstone belatedly answered Gooper, "Th' detonator's got a battery an' a radio receiver. It's triggered by a particular radio frequency resonance that—"

Gooper cut him off. "Ow, shaddap! I don't want ter build me own! You rigged a bomb. That's wot I need ter know."

"I was worried I wouldn't be able to place it, but all the sick guards today made it easy," Tombstone said.

Quack worked steadily, snipping away at the thick wires by sense of touch.

Tombstone unslung his duffel bag. "Here, Gooper. Hold this bag. I'll get the transmitter out now. It's short-range. B'fore we get into the woods, I'd best fire it off."

"We are so very, very visible, sahibs," Sam said in strained tones.

Bert murmured, "We'll be through the fence soon, Sam."

Every few seconds a click announced another link of chain fence defeated. Tombstone rummaged for his transmitter, then held it cupped in his hands. It looked like a battery with a rat's nest of wires tied on. Tombstone twisted a pair of wires together. "It's all ready. I just got t' press this here key down."

Quack said, "I'm through! Tombstone, come on. You and your transmitter are next."

The lanky Texan squeezed through the rent in the fence. Sam was next.

Gooper got stuck.

"Ow, bloody 'ell!" The massive man tried to bull through. Then he tried to go back. The whole fence quivered with his efforts, but the flexible chain gave him little purchase for his powerful muscles.

"Wait. What was that? Was that a shot fired just now?" Tombstone wondered, much quieter than the protesting Gooper.

Bert, alone on the inside of the fence, was amused. "Quack, get back here and snip some more. You underestimated a bit."

"Mebbe a pistol shot," Tombstone said.

A quivery light fell upon them all. It was the dim light of a battery-powered torch, but it seemed as bright as the sun. A German-accented voice shouted, "Halt!" Footsteps pounded nearer.

Bert turned to face the light, a wild, tight smile on his face. "Well, if it isn't my old friend, Uwe." Bert walked toward the light, then broke into a run.

"Halten sie!" came Uwe's voice. Then the torch dropped to the ground, casting a cone of light in a direction useless to everyone.

A shot rang out.

Bert gave a cry.

"Bert's been hit!" howled Gooper, still stuck in the fence.

CHAPTER 10

Ace walked with straight-backed dignity into the house. Darko Dor's musclebound bodyguard jabbed his gun barrel between her shoulder blades. He smiled when Ace stumbled and emitted an involuntary gasp. He exuded a chilling aura of uncaring brutality.

Darko Dor met them inside the house. No wine was in sight, this time, though he wore a pleased half-smile. "Ah, Miss Carroway. So good of you to join us."

"Look," Ace said, her golden eyes glinting, "whatever it is, the answer's going to be 'no.' Give up, Darko Dor."

"I would give up, my dear. Except that I don't. I never give up. I knew you would be defiant, Miss Carroway. It is part of your charm. It is why I admire you so." Darko Dor stroked his little goatee with smug contractions of his fingers.

Ace stood encased in silent tension.

The government minister lost his smile, irritated at the lack of response. "My work here is done. The *Falke* is on track for production. I am leaving. And you are coming with me."

"In a pig's eye!"

"Ha! Ha! Ha! So charming. So very fiery." Darko Dor chuckled. He indicated the hulking bodyguard. "Miss Carroway, meet Cherenkov. He is most fearsome, yes? Let me be clear. You have no choice. You have no luggage, and ours is packed. We are leaving for Frankfurt now. Cherenkov cares not if you are awake or unconscious, healthy or bleeding. I have told him I want you alive, but I did not otherwise restrict him. Cherenkov likes his artistic freedom, you see."

Cherenkov ran the barrel of his large-bore pistol over the back of Ace's neck. A cold, sickly caress. Ace shuddered.

"I see that you understand your situation, Miss Carroway. Let us go. Now!"

Ace went with the men into the inky night. At the fading edge of the porch light's circle of illumination sat Darko's official car. Long, black, and gleaming, it was built to impress. Broad running boards, four doors with tinted glass windows, and an imposing front grill added to the effect.

Darko Dor went to the driver's side. "Put her in the back seat and watch her!" The Ottoman Minister started to get in. Cherenkov opened the back door of the sedan and gestured for Ace to get in too.

She did not obey.

Instead of ducking to get into the car, she crouched into a *Wing Chun* stance. The next instant, she leapt and delivered a high kick to the base of Cherenkov's skull. The bodyguard's eyes glazed and crossed. He weaved on his feet. Ace doubled him over with a stomach punch, then helped in his downward trajectory with a two-handed smash to the back of the neck. His face impacted the solid fender, and his head bounced off. By the time Cherenkov's boneless form reached the ground, he was unconscious. Breathing hard, Ace looked for Darko Dor.

She found him, standing behind a steady Luger pistol. His dark eyes glittered.

"You try my patience!" His snarling voice quivered. "Get in the driver's seat. You will drive me."

"No," Ace panted.

Darko Dor lowered his gun, but not to give up. In an act of callous, indifferent cruelty he pointed the Luger at Cherenkov's head and pulled the trigger. The gun emitted a crisp pop sound and a flash of muzzle fire.

Ace emitted a soft cry of protest, jarred, but slow to fully comprehend the barren inhumanity of the casual murder.

Darko Dor's teeth gleamed in the gloom. "Interesting. I have understood your weakness now, Ace Carroway. If you do not get in, I will have your fellow prisoners shot, one by one. And you will watch them die, one by one. Move."

Dislocated from reality and nerveless, Ace trembled as she slipped behind the wheel. Mechanically, she turned the key and trimmed the choke.

Darko Dor stepped over what was once Cherenkov and into the back seat. "Never doubt, my dear, this gun is aimed at your heart." His voice slithered intimately behind her right ear.

From outside came a crack sound, a distant gun shot. It was so like an echo that Ace at first thought it was her own imagination. But the shot brought her back to her right self, and she knew where she was and what she was doing.

A memory flitted by.

"In improvisation, Cecilia, there are infinitely many paths to take, and you are the master of them all," said Chathaway Monahan, her piano tutor. An established concert pianist, posters often featured his image. Cecilia was 11.

"But don't I have to follow the chord progression and end on the tonic?" Cecilia looked over and up at the dashing figure. *Sometimes, she asked questions just to see his reactions. More often, she begged him to play so that she could be transported to musical landscapes only he could conjure.*

"Of course. You still have to get around the changes and navigate the cadence to the end of the form. But I'm still right. You know I'm right, don't you, you scamp?"

"Yes, Mister Monahan. Mathematically, but also for mood."

"Scamp. What do you know of mood at your age? But you are right. Your end goal can be achieved, in style. In your own style."

Her eyes grew metallic. She put the car in gear and accelerated.

Darko Dor loomed behind her, an unseen yet vivid compulsion. Ace was keenly aware that he had a pistol pointed at her heart. She drove toward the exit gate, trying to think. She recited a *Wing Chun* mantra, calming her breath, clarifying her mind.

Darko Dor purred, "There. See? You can be reasonable, my dear. Now, it is only a mile to the highway."

Suddenly, the sky behind them turned bright orange. Ace saw an expanding ball of flame in her rearview mirror. It dimmed and curled and rose into a mushroom shape.

"Was zur Hölle?"[10] blurted Darko Dor. He commanded, "Turn around! Turn around!"

Ace was already turning. Tires spit dirt and gravel as she spun the car and accelerated. The rutty country

---

[10] What the hell?

road made the smooth-riding Ministry car bounce crazily. Ace kept her foot nailed to the floor.

As they careened past the farmhouse again, the flames from the fuel depot came into view, with silhouetted running figures. But Ace seemed to be drifting from that course and heading more toward the barn. At ever increasing speed.

Darko Dor noticed. *"Was zur Hölle?"* he shouted again. "Stop! Go that way!"

Ace angled the car between house and barn. In the light of car's vibrating headlights, she spotted a slash in the chain-link fence. She headed toward it, her foot pressing the accelerator flat. For a moment, there was a lump in the field and the car bounced severely. Had the car run over a body?

"I will shoot you!" Darko Dor screamed.

"Think twice about that, Ottoman. We'll both die if you do!" Ace said, voice unyielding as solid metal.

The car split the chain-link fence with a wallop that slowed it momentarily and tore off a headlight. Ace steered straight for the forest, eyes straining to see in the wildly jiggling rays of the one remaining headlight.

"Ha! There is no escape for you! Forget you, madwoman! I wash my hands of you and your crazy American ideals ... Ahhh! Watch out! The tree!"

Ace was doing nothing *but* watching the tree. This was going to be some tricky driving.

The thick tree stood alone at the edge of the forest. Ace kept accelerating to the very end. The tree loomed larger and larger. Darko Dor screamed. His gun went off, but the bullet punctured a hole in the center of the windshield. He had aimed at the tree in his panic.

Ace suddenly twisted the steering wheel. The car

turned sideways amid a shower of dirt. Broadside, it struck the tree. There was a booming crash of metal and a shattering explosion of glass. And then all went quiet.

Very quiet.

Lifelessly quiet.

Chapter 11

Bert was shot. The numbing sting tore through his shoulder and staggered him as he ran toward Uwe. Uwe clicked another cartridge into place in his gun, but by then Bert was there, in agony, true, but also at the very peak of rage. Bert had one good arm, and he used it, punching Uwe in the face with all his pent-up frustration and anger. Uwe was bowled over backwards by the terrific punch, his rifle falling from nerveless fingers.

Bert stood there panting, feeling warm wetness spread down his ribs.

Belatedly, he told the limp body, "Eh … take *that*! Ha!" and reached down to take Uwe's rifle.

Bert staggered back to the fence. "Bumbling, comedic pack of dolts! This is no way to win a war! A shot has been fired! The camp is probably about to be swarming with guards, and Ace is still—"

"Bert." Quack was at his elbow, his voice full of concern. "Come on. We got Gooper unstuck. So sorry. You got your man, though. By the thunder of the Wakinyan,[11] I think you broke his face!"

Bert chuckled, pleased. "Heh. I did, didn't I? I didn't know I had it in me!"

Sam had the presence of mind to retrieve Uwe's electric torch. He snapped it off, then hurried to join

---

[11] The thunderbirds of the Lakota People.

the retreat.

They moved on until they were at the edge of the woods.

Quack begged, "Let's stop, please. And listen for pursuit. And … see if Ace is coming."

"An' blow up the fuel," Tombstone said.

Bert said, "Yah, yah! Blow up the — Ow! Ow! Stop!"

Quack handled Bert's pierced shoulder. "Hush. I'm a doctor. We have to stop the bleeding. We'll get the bullet out later." Quack was as gentle as he could be, in the dark. He ripped the blood-wet coverall over the bullet hole with his fingers. He undid his own coverall far enough to get to his undershirt, then hastily ripped it until he managed to make strips. He crudely bound Bert's injury.

Bert jabbered dizzily. "You are not a doctor, sir! You were barely enrolled in medical school when the war broke out! Why else should I call you a quack? It's only the truth."

Meanwhile, Tombstone triggered his radio trans-mitter. Then triggered it again. Then a third, fourth, and fifth time, saying, "Aw, nuts, I don't think it—"

The sky turned orange. The fuel dump turned into a fireball, which dimmed and rose and curled into a mushroom shape.

"D'awww, now hain't that a beautiful sight!" Gooper sighed lyrically. A second later, the thudding concussion made him smile even larger.

Quack said, "Beautiful, indeed! Plus, it let me see what I was doing for a second. That bandage will have to do for now, Bert."

"Thanks, friend."

"Gentlemen, I do not see any guards coming this way, but what is that engine?" Sam said.

Soon they all could see and hear. A black Ministry sedan skidded and swerved its wild way between house and barn, heading toward them.

"Ace?" wondered Sam.

"Ace! C'mon, Ace!" cheered Bert through teeth clenched against the pain of his bullet wound.

They all laughed with relief and cheered as the car burst through the chain-link fence and headed, as it seemed, straight for them.

"Erm," Gooper said.

"Um. Slow down, Ace!" Quack urged.

"She will crash! She will crash!" Sam bleated.

The car ran straight at a large tree, but at the last second, the wheels turned and the car slid sideways. It might have started tumbling and rolling had the tree not been there, but with a bone-rattling crash, it came to a very, very abrupt halt.

As the sounds of tinkling glass faded, the men ran toward the scene. Sam had Uwe's electric torch. He played it upon the wreckage. The car had struck the tree broadside, at the level of the back seat. The light illuminated a crumpled form. It was a body, covered in glass, bark, and blood.

"Lady Ace?" inquired Sam in choked tones. "But no, that is the minister!" He reoriented his light.

In the driver's seat, a woozy, bruised Ace smiled fuzzily at them. "Up here, fellas. My door's stuck. Help a girl out?"

Gooper guffawed. "Wif pleasure!" He put a hand on the door handle and gave a mighty yank. Metal bent, and the door yielded to Gooper's bunched muscles. He handed Ace out like a gallant prince of old.

"You crashed on purpose, to get rid of that guy?" Quack inquired.

"Yes. I didn't have a lot of options. He had a gun on me. Oof! I hurt all over, but we can't stay."

"I should say not!" Sam agreed.

"Inter th' woods, then! We can make a few miles before sunup," Gooper said.

They melted away into the night trees.

They traversed steep slopes in the darkness, weaving in and around barely-seen trees. Ace and Bert were both dizzy and weak, and the other three helped them along through the obstacles.

Gooper lectured them as they walked, feeling in high spirits. "Now, don't yew fret about hounds. The thing about trained hounds is they've got ter 'ave a scent ter start off with. If they just release hounds at the start of our trail, the hounds are goin' ter chase squirrels an' rabbits, not us. Mind you, we stink to 'igh 'eaven. So one thing ter do is ter find a clean stream to bathe in."

"It's last quarter moon. The moon should be rising in about an hour," Ace said. "Head more west for now. The terrain's more rugged. We'll turn north later on."

The moon rose as Ace predicted. Its wan light helped to navigate the increasingly precarious paths.

"Mah boots are fallin' apart," Tombstone fretted.

"I can help when we stop," Quack said. "I stole some leather scraps."

Ace grew stronger as the night wore on, but Bert flagged. "Look for shelter, Gooper," Ace said.

"Yeah. I'm down to socks fer shoes now," Tombstone said.

But it was Sam that spotted something. He patted Gooper on the meaty arm and pointed. "Sahib. Down there. It is a limestone cave, I think."

Gooper peered and said, "It hain't but a hole in the ground."

"Please allow me the benefit of the doubt, sahib. This is Karst topography," Sam cryptically insisted, leading the way.

The cave entrance was indeed little more than a hole, but it opened into a vast chamber. Gooper turned on the feeble electric torch and played it on the walls.

"Cor!" he gasped.

The rest stared, too. Ghostly stains decorated the walls, painstakingly applied by the hands of artists that lived millennia before the dawn of recorded history. Deer, bears, bison, mammoths, sabretooth cats, and stick figures of people paraded across the limestone.

"Who's got the rifle?" Quack inquired.

"Sahib, I do!" said Sam with an air of surprise. He couldn't remember who had handed it to him, or when.

"How many bullets does it have?"

Sam opened the breach. "Ah. Three, sahib. Three bullets."

"You take first watch, Sam. Wake me for second watch." Quack was helping Bert to nest. The floor was a loamy soil with large divots the right size to sleep in all curled up. Bert sank into one with a faint groan and closed his eyes, immediately falling into an exhausted slumber.

"These 'ere dimples in the floor are bear beds!" sunnily announced Gooper. He looked around to see many eyes looking roundly at him. He amended, "Erm, *old* bear beds. Old ones. Th' cave'd be all smelly if bears were livin' here now."

Tombstone said, "Y'all git yerself a bear bed then, and turn off the torch. Save the battery."

The darkness that came was absolute. In the cool and quiet the Allies fell comatose. Sam heroically kept his eyes open, but nothing, not even a bear, came to disturb them.

Chapter 12

Gradually, they came awake. Afternoon sun diffused into the cave. From time to time, the buzz of an airplane rose and fell.

"Lookin' fer us, mebbe," Tombstone said. He had squirreled away a couple of metal cans in his duffel. Gooper took them and left the cave to find water. Ace exercised, dauntlessly stretching despite deep bruises.

Quack watched Gooper from the tiny cave entrance. "It is odd. Somehow, he blends into the scenery. His red hair is like the red leaves. His pale skin is like birch bark."

Tombstone said, "He's so wrong he ends up right? Typical."

Gooper returned with spring water and pockets bulging with walnuts. Bert was parched, and Gooper had to make two trips more before everybody's thirst was slaked.

Quack took Tombstone's boots and looked them over. "They're done for, Tombstone. But don't worry. I have enough leather to make you moccasins."

"You kin do that? Where'd you learn that?"

Quack drafted the wire cutters into service as shoemaker tools. "I'm part Sioux."

"Huh? But you're blond."

"*Part* Sioux. My grandfather was a Swede. My mother had blond hair." Quack settled down to leatherworking. "What's Karst topography, Sam?"

Sam answered readily. "It is land built with the rock called limestone, sahib. It makes for steep canyons, and sinkholes, and caves like this one."

Ace cracked walnuts, then passed the nutmeats around, hand to hand. She said, "Can you tell us about the cave paintings?"

"I am afraid not, Lady Ace. The paintings are older than written history. In my mind, they *are* written history, but written in pictures. You can see that the artists knew animals that no longer roam the earth. The mammoth. The sabretooth cat. The cave bear."

Tombstone said, "Shewt. We think we got it tough. Jes' think about them cave people. Even if they hunted a critter, next thing you know they'd be fightin' t' keep it against sabretooth cats or giant bears!"

"Probably drove them a bit," Ace popped a walnut into her mouth, "nuts."

Bert grinned. "Very punny."

"Bert? We never got your full name, or how you ended up a prisoner."

Quack wheedled, "Tell them, Bert. If you don't, I'll tell lies about you."

"Very well. My given name is Hubert Ewing Devery Christopher Bostock the Third. One of the Boston Bostocks, if you know East Coast society."

"Ah shore don't," Tombstone drawled.

Bert said, "Good! I like life better when unburdened by expectations. But my branch of the family strayed from tradition anyway. My father was a doctor, and he squandered his inheritance to try to bring modern medicine to remote parts of the world. He met my mother in Panama, and that is where they live. I had trouble choosing a career. I had my own interests—"

"Namely, chasing girls," Quack inserted.

Bert did not bother to deny it. "I ended up studying law. I had just passed my bar exam when the war broke out. I was earning my officer stripes when Quack ruined my life, but I'll let him tell that part."

"Oh? All right. Quack?" Ace said.

"You shyster," Quack said darkly. "My name is Boxnard Warburton Snana. That last name is Lakota Sioux. Growing up, I split my time between South Dakota and Boston. I know Bert from Harvard."

Bert interrupted. "That's Hahvahd."

"...often mispronounced Hahvahd. We were on the fencing team together. Take it from me, he was a donkey's rear end back then, too. When the war broke out, I was in medical school. That is why they made me a field medic."

"Get to the good stuff," Bert urged, "such as sending me a letter so full of lies you should be court-martialed."

"Well, I did imply that there were pretty girls. And there were, but they were orphans, not date material for Bert. They needed rescuing. The trouble was, this orphanage was in Luxembourg, and that's behind enemy lines. I needed an officer's approval to do anything, and I knew Bert was an officer, or trying to be. So, yes, I sent a letter. To his credit, he came to see me."

"Then he got me drunk!" Bert said.

"Then I got us both so drunk that neither one of us could see straight. We dressed up in coveralls like delivery men. We took a motorcycle with a sidecar and tried to drive to Luxembourg. Somehow, we thought that our disguises would fool the border guards. They did not. We were captured."

"Yeah, imagine!" Bert snickered. He turned to Ace. "So where do we go next?"

Everyone looked at Ace. It seemed natural. It was more than the fact that Ace always seemed several steps ahead. It was more than the fact that Ace had laid three of them in the dirt in the space of a heartbeat. It transcended the twin oddities that the leader of the group would be the youngest and the only female. It was a simple sense of harmony, almost like music. It was the configuration that made the engine run smooth and powerful.

Ace was the carburetor, injecting the right mix of fuel and air into the conversation. "I was shot down over Verviers, and what I saw there gives me an idea. Maybe we don't have to walk all the way to France."

"What did you see, Lady Ace?" said Sam.

"Outside Verviers there are brand new airship hangars. They are very large and very secret. Like the *Falke*, I bet it's something new the Ottomans are cooking up. Verviers is not far. My guess is it's about twenty miles from here, almost due north. What would you say if I proposed stealing an airship and flying home in it?"

"Wot? Stealin'? Us?" Gooper said with exaggerated innocence.

"New, experimental airships, eh?" Bert mused.

"Lots of secrecy, then. Lots of guards with lots of guns." Quack tapped a wise finger on his temple.

"A closely watched, highly secure area, most assuredly." Sam nodded.

"Blinkin' suicide mission ter try to take a whole airship!" Gooper grinned.

"Oh, and a long journey there on foot, through enemy territory crawling with soldiers," Bert said.

Tombstone drawled, "Ma'am? Let me offer a translation on behalf o' my cohorts. All of that means: We're in, and when do we start?"

Chapter 13

The party left the prehistoric painted cave and forged ahead through autumn forests that hugged Belgian ridges. Tombstone padded along gratefully in moccasins. They ducked under cover at the sound of airplanes. Once, they dodged a group of four armed soldiers. They hid in an overgrown ditch. After a tense quarter-hour, the soldiers went away. A sweating Tombstone whispered, "Lookin' fer us, do ya think?"

Ace said, "Probably not. They'd expect us to go west, not north. There's a war on, too. They can't spare too many soldiers for backwoods chases."

They crept north. As shadows lengthened on the forested slopes, they heard distant gunshots. They froze.

"Resistance fighters," Quack said.

"Right," Bert said.

"There are many that would rather die than march to orders issued from Istanbul," Sam said.

They huddled to discuss strategy. Quack and Ace were concerned about lead poisoning from Bert's bullet. Gooper chimed in and vividly described how bacterial infections grow exponentially. Bert maintained that he could keep going indefinitely, but he looked pale. He was overruled.

"That bullet's got to come out," said Ace.

Still miles short of Verviers, they selected a lonely farm. It lay near the end of one of the cultivated valleys that poked like fingers between forested mountain ridges. Dusk fell.

"Who besides me speaks French?" Ace asked.

Shifty-eyed looks crisscrossed the group.

"Perhaps if it were written down," Sam said.

"You are it, Ace," Quack said.

Ace stripped off her greasy mechanic coveralls to reveal her bloodstained aviator suit. It was recognizably Allied, though the insignia had been torn off. As the others lurked out of sight, Ace knocked on the door.

A sober couple answered. A small boy peeped out from between them. After a few minutes of conversation, Ace beckoned the men out of hiding. "Come on out, fellas. These are the Knoxes. Their elder son was taken by the Ottomans. They're eager to help. We talked about risk, but they don't mind us staying for a day. They say the soldiers don't come by very often."

The Knoxes and the Allies bowed and smiled to each other across the language barrier.

The next item of business was bullet extraction.

Ace and Quack scrounged for improvised instruments and supplies. They boiled their tools to sterilize them. The living room transformed into an operating theater. Quack handed Bert a bottle of whisky and said, "Permission to get glassy-eyed granted."

"Permission? I outrank you, Quack," said Bert.

"So order yourself to do it, then!" Quack turned to Ace. "Who's doing what? You were further along than I was in medical school."

"I can do the extraction," Ace said, cool as a cave.

"Done! I'll assist. I was more interested in psychology anyway. So, you've done surgeries like this before?"

Ace said, "I read about it. It should be straightforward."

Quack blinked. "You just — read about it."

Bert groaned and drank faster.

When Bert began to slur his words, the operation began. Tombstone held a kerosene lamp high to give light. The rest made a curious ring, including the Knoxes' younger son, eyes wide as saucers.

Ace located the bullet by palpating his shoulder with gentle fingertips. The bullet had passed most of the way through Bert's shoulder, coming to rest a knuckle-width below the skin on the far side. Ace made a precise, inch-long incision. By sense of touch or some mysterious sixth sense, Ace reached sterile needle-nosed pliers into the oozing incision, and extracted the bullet in one smooth motion. Quack was ready with a whisky-soaked swab, followed by needle and thread to suture the skin shut. Bert bit on a rag to keep from screaming, tears running down his face. After Quack wrapped him with clean bandages, Bert removed the rag and quavered, "I hate you and love you at the same time."

♠♠♠

Everyone slept late into next morning. Mrs. Knox woke them by announcing it was bath time and handed them all towels to wrap themselves with. Ace got Mrs. Knox's housecoat. The sunburst of joy and gratitude from the Allies made the Knoxes laugh and smile.

While they bathed, Mrs. Knox washed their clothes.

Clean, but waiting for her coveralls to dry, Ace wandered into a walled herb garden at the back of the house. Keeping an ear open for airplanes, she relaxed on a small bench. Patches of sunlight brought fleeting warmth to the chilly, cloud-speckled October day. Ten-year-old Pietr Knox crept out of the house and approached Ace tentatively.

Ace spoke in French. "Pietr. You look like you have something on your mind."

Pietr hesitated. Ace patted the seat beside her.

Pietr plopped down. Forgetting his shyness, he piped, "I want to fly airplanes when I grow up!"

"And why is that?"

"I like airplanes! And the Ottomans are bad. They took Rolf and all our cattle, and they frightened us. I want to kill them."

Ace replied soberly, "Will killing them solve anything?

Pietr thought for a moment. "It will end the war."

"Yes. But, Pietr, that is all. Once the war is over, there no point to killing. More killing after the war is over would only make things worse."

Pietr stuck out his lower jaw. "I still want to be a pilot!"

Ace laughed. "Good! Give me another reason you want to!"

"I want to fly in the air!"

"Ah, that's a better reason. There's nothing like flying."

"Maybe someday we will fly to the moon!" Pietr bounced in his seat.

"Well. I never thought of that. Maybe you can."

"And I want to be just like you, Madame!"

"Now you've gone too far! Take this sprig of rosemary with you and go help peel potatoes, you little fox!" Ace shooed the grinning boy off.

There was a lot of potato-peeling going on in the kitchen. Five men dressed in towels chopped cabbage, simmered chicken stock, and peeled and cubed potatoes. Except Bert. Bert was leaning on the kitchen door frame, holding his head. He was hung over.

"Voici le romarin!" Pietr piped, weaving through the lumpy maze of legs, holding up his herb.

"Rosemary?" rumbled Gooper. "Well, now. Hain't that a good idea! 'Oo thought o' that, I wonder?" He added the sprig to the queue of things to be chopped.

"Captain Carroway, no doubt," Quack said.

"Captain Flying Ace Carroway," said Tombstone.

"Keep it down, yah?" Bert pleaded, holding his head.

Stirring and chopping sounds filled the rustic kitchen. Bert raised his head and looked blearily at the motley collection of paradoxically appealing misfits. "So, erm," he began hesitantly. They all looked at him. Bert lost his nerve and said instead, "So, Ace. She's underage."

Quack said, "Yes. Maybe explains part of why she likes to keep a low profile. She doesn't want to be sent home."

Sam said, "I think you are right, Quack. However, we should not dwell on it. Until we escape back to France, there are more pressing problems."

"Yup." Tombstone nodded at Sam.

Bert steeled himself, then forged ahead. "But what do you *think* of her?"

The stirring and chopping sounds stopped as everyone considered the simple-sounding but profound question. The silence stretched.

Finally, Quack said, "She's Ace!"

There was a general meeting of eyes and nods of accord. The chopping and stirring resumed.

When the Allies got their coveralls back, they were not only washed, but also dyed a dark brown. Mr. Knox proudly distributed the garments to a chorus of appreciation from all. The new color was much better for staying hidden than the original white, even considering the grease stains and slathered muck.

When everyone was dressed again, Ace cornered Tombstone. "What's left in your bag of wires, Tombstone? Any more bombs?"

"Ah reckon not, ma'am," Tombstone answered dolefully. "Th' vacuum tubes broke in the escape. The battery Ah used in the transmitter is iffy, but there's a spare. Ah got an 'lectric speaker, lots o' wire, resistors an' capacitors . . ."

Ace was silent for a minute, then snapped her fingers. "That'll be good enough! You can make a timer using RC circuits. We'll need ten or fifteen minutes on the timer. Then it needs to trigger the solenoid you're going to build out of the loudspeaker. The solenoid core will bump a hair-trigger brace. Without the brace, the wire cutters will snap closed. All we are missing is a thick spring."

Tombstone struggled to keep up. "Uh, you want a timer that triggers an electromagnet, and then a wire gets cut?"

"That's right. Like a mousetrap. A tiny touch, then, *snap*! I'll build the mousetrap. You build the timer that makes the solenoid core go bump."

Ace did not waste time. Their stay in the cozy house would end at sundown, and it was already afternoon. She slipped out into the gray day furtively, eyes and ears alert for anything moving. She ducked into a shed and blinked.

Gooper was sitting in there, a cat on his lap. Another cat rode his shoulders. His thick finger caressed the chin of a third sitting near, its feline eyes half closed in bliss.

Gooper looked up at Ace, pale face flushing red. "Oy, Oy was just, err …"

Ace fought back a smile. "I don't see any cats. None at all. You've come to help me look for a spring."

"Aye. A spring. That'll be the thing."

Ace returned to the house carrying a rusty but sturdy spring and the broken leg of a chair. The farmers gifted the useless junk to the escaping Allies with a shrug and a laugh.

Ace affixed the stiff spring across the wire nipper handles. She whittled the hardwood of the broken chair leg to prop the device open. The wooden prop slipped out very easily. When propped open, delicately but under great tension, the nippers became fearsome. Ace tested it by wedging a thick stick into the jaws. With the lightest of touches, the jaws snapped shut and the stick popped into two pieces.

Tombstone happened to witness it, and commented, "Tarnation!"

Bert appeared in the doorway, standing steady and looking only slightly pale. "Supper's ready!"

Chapter 14

Darkness fell. There were handshakes and hugs and farewells, but not many dry eyes. The Allies hiked off toward Verviers dressed in brown. Bert said he felt like a new man.

About ten miles and two forested ridges later, Bert retracted his opinion. "I'm gassed! Can we take a rest?"

"No need. We're here," Ace said over her shoulder. "Peek around the next trees. We're still high up on the ridge, but you'll see the base."

The Allies hunkered down and peered out. Electric light made the fantastic scene more eerie. Five airship hangers loomed like monstrous pill bugs lined up at a drinking trough, dominating the regular hangars.

Gray traces of dawn tinged the eastern sky. Larks sang welcome to the day's beginning, ignorant of matters of war. At the hangars, dotlike workers wheeled out two airships. Majestically the ribbed, rigid giants rolled forward, emerging from their cocoons into the electric light. Beneath the gas bag two gondolas hung like metal shoes with windows. When the angled tail fins cleared the hangars, rows of propeller-capped engine cars belched smoke and roared to life.

"They are gigantic!" Sam breathed.

Ace's narrowed eyes studied them. "More engine cars than I've ever seen! Eight of them, it looks like. That means speed. The forward gondola is for the crew. The rear one … I'm guessing that's for bombs. I see machine guns in the rear. I think it does not dock at a mast. It sits on its own wheels. It must have a ground anchor of some kind."

"They're bombers?" Quack said.

"Long-range bombers," Ace answered grimly. "Probably thousands of miles of range. They could strike anywhere in Europe."

As daylight brightened, the airships prepared to launch. The hidden Allies watched the stately behemoths leave the ground and float off into the morning sky.

"Ah didn't see 'em loadin' any ordnance on board," Tombstone said.

"What is ordnance, sahib?" Sam asked.

"Bombs an' ammo," Tombstone said.

Bert said, "Are there just the two airships, or all five? Maybe they are making test flights, or observation flights."

Quack said, "Ace? What's the plan, anyway?"

Ace replied, "Plan A is to cut the power in the middle of the night so the electric lights go out. Tombstone and I built a timer hooked to the wire cutter. With the lights out, we can sneak into an airship unseen. Hopefully, we can fire up the engines and go. With the moon waning, the night will be dark. In the best of all possible worlds, it would be nice to have a diversion. This is a military base, and everyone down there has a gun. They have trucks mounted with machine guns. They probably have big guns ... yes, see? There, and there." Ace pointed. "They have cannon made to shoot airplanes."

"Did yew say *diversion*?" Gooper tasted the word in his mouth as if it were fine wine.

"Whoa, there, dogie!" Tombstone said, motioning to shush Gooper.

Ace said, "No, it's all right. Let's have everybody's ideas."

Sam said, "What sort of thing would make them roll out all the airships?"

Bert said, "An inspection?"

Sam said, "Possibly."

Bert blurted, "An attack!" He deflated. "But we probably can't manage that."

Quack said, "Could we come close? Could we make the air raid sirens go off? Assuming they have air raid sirens, that is."

"Ow, let's just find where they keep the bombs and blow 'em up!" Gooper was impatient.

Ace said, "Hold up, Gooper. Having the regular crews roll out the dirigibles solves a lot of problems. We would stow away, then overpower the crew once we are in clear air."

"Well, blowing up the munitions wouldn't 'urt anything! It'd make the attack more believable," Gooper cajoled.

Ace scanned the scene microscopically.

A low, haunting warble tickled the ears. It was impossible to locate the source. Most of the men looked around at the trees. Sam's eyes fell on Ace. The sound died.

Ace said, "Gooper, I'm about to make your day. Do you see the building almost hidden in the trees? It's on the near corner, close to us and very far from everything else. That's got to be where they keep the explosives. There's nowhere else that makes sense. Not by all the planes and their hangars. Not by the airships and their hangars. It's right there by the forest edge."

"I am purrin' like a kitten!" Gooper admitted, wringing his hands in anticipation.

Tombstone said, "Aw, don't encourage the Limey. Not that Ah object to explosions. Ah kinda like 'em."

Ace was subdued. "The bad news is we only have one timer. We can rig it to tap a detonator inside that building, but if we do, we can't cut the electricity."

"I can't spot the power wires anyway, Ace," Quack said. "Except 'way over there, north toward Verviers itself, there is a row of poles. I think the cables must be buried."

Bert said, "I hate to agree with the Quack, but he's right on this one."

"Fair enough. Power outage is demoted to Plan B. For now, let's stay and watch. There will be patrols around the perimeter. We need to time them."

They watched. They discovered that there was always a patrol. It consisted of four guards. They strolled ceaselessly around the inside of the fence that enclosed the airport. The perimeter was so vast that it took them half an hour to make one round.

"They will notice a hole in the fence," Sam said, "Therefore, in less than thirty minutes of us getting in, there will be an alarm."

Quack said, "Say! I have an idea! We can pose as that unit of guards, and walk around the inside of the fence right to the airship hangars. From a distance, we'd look the same, just a group of people."

"You like to impersonate people, Quack," Bert said. "I remember that from Harvard."

Ace said, "I think we've seen enough for now. Let's

try to get a little sleep."

CHAPTER 15

They slept fitfully up a convenient ravine, invisible under blankets of colorful dry leaves. Warplanes buzzed overhead frequently, landing and taking off. In the afternoon, they gave up on sleep. Quack patiently extracted drinking water from a hillside seep, but only a few nuts could be found to eat. Ace removed the hinge from the heavy wire cutters, separating the tool into a pair of awkward axes. She handed the implements to Gooper and Quack. "Pick a slender log with branches still attached. Not too slender. It has to hold Gooper's weight. Chop off the branches on top and bottom, and make the sideways ones stubby."

"What for?" Quack was mystified.

"A ladder, you Quack-pot!" Bert smugly informed him. "You made such a mess of the last fence that this time we're just climbing over it."

Quack said, "Wipe that smirk off your face, Brat, or I'll wipe it off for you!"

After the crude ladder was shaped, Gooper tested it out, climbing a walnut tree and scoring a few more nuts. The ladder did not break.

Ace harvested a sapling. She trimmed off the branches and lopped off the top. The sapling became a slender pole about twelve feet long.

Sam said, "What is that for, Lady Ace?"

Ace said, "Clear me a path." Holding the pole in front of her, she accelerated forward in an open lane between trees. She planted the pole into the ground. The sapling bent as her forward momentum was transformed to upward flight. Ace flew ten feet in the air before letting go of the pole and wheeling her arms for a crouch landing.

"Pole vault!" exclaimed Tombstone.

Then they all scrambled for cover. Warplanes droned overhead on a landing approach.

Before sunset, the Allies crept back to scout the airport some more. They brought their makeshift ladder and pole. This time, they came to the edge of the forest, a stone's throw from the building they thought held bombs and munitions. It was isolated, ventilated, unremarkable.

They spotted the air raid horns. They were mechanical, not electric. To operate them, one grasped a handle at the back and gave a few hearty turns. They would wail like banshees.

"I see two sirens. No more," Sam said.

"Yep," agreed Tombstone. "One's 'way across the airstrip by the airplane hangars where we ain't goin'. An' the other's past the farthest airship hangar, where we also ain't goin'."

Bert mournfully observed, "You know your plan is in trouble when the *easiest* option is exploding the ordnance storage."

"Hush. Here comes the patrol again," Quack whispered.

Slothlike, the sun sank into a cloud bank near the western horizon. Evening twilight crept grudgingly into the sky.

It was agony for the raw-nerved Allies to wait, but they knew their false air raid would be more plausible at midnight. They had no choice. They waited, gritting their teeth against the jagged, twitchy impulse to leap into action.

Night fell, starry and cold. The Allies maintained their vigil as the hours crawled by.

Ace broke the strained silence. "Fellas. I would like to say, whatever happens next, I was lucky to meet you. I never had anybody just accept me the way I was before. You fellas are terrific."

Assorted hems and haws rumbled.

Tombstone said, "Aww, Ace! Yer— Get down!"

Headlights swept across their position outside the perimeter fence. They got low behind their respective tree trunks. After a while, they peeked. A laden flatbed truck rolled right up to the bomb bunker. It unhurriedly seesawed to get turned around backwards. It backed up to the building, very gently. The engine shut off.

The Allies could not see the action very well from their location behind the building. They caught glimpses of two men in officer's caps silhouetted against the electric lights of the distant field. The officers cast long shadows. Faint sounds of locks being opened, chains being unwound, and latches being released wafted through the air to the tense six. This went on for quite a while.

"Lots o' locks!" Gooper whispered, impressed.

The ordnance officers labored. Time stretched. The Allies wondered and waited, cramped and tense. Carts rolled. Chains jingled. Conversational voices murmured. The four-soldier perimeter patrol came by, and for a few minutes the voices grew louder, calling greetings, joking, and chatting. After a prickly eternity the patrol went on its way again.

The foot patrol turned the corner and headed for the airplane hangars. Ace whispered, "We can't let them lock up again. Follow me."

Before the men could say a word, Ace was thumping off at a dead run. They heard a quiet *chuff* sound as her pole planted in the gravelly turf. They saw her silhouette poised against the starry sky, her body arcing dolphinlike over the razor wire loops. The men heard the pole drop back to earth, but they did not see Ace in the dense shadow cast by the ordnance bunker.

So abrupt had been Ace's departure, it took a few moments for the men to move, but their rickety ladder was ready. They skulked forward. Tombstone and Gooper carried the ladder. They eased it to the top of the fence. It was long enough, barely, to depress the top curl of barbed wire with a metallic whisper. According to plan, Bert was the first to climb because of his weak arm. The others held the ladder steady for him.

When Bert was halfway up, he was suddenly illuminated from the right. Five pairs of eyes snapped to the direction of the source.

"Car!" hissed Quack.

"Hide!" said Sam.

Bert jumped down. The men scrambled back to the first rank of trees. They abandoned the ladder. A small armored truck came bouncing around the outside of the fence. Its headlights lit up the leaning log. At the ladder, the truck graveled to a stop. Dust clouded in the beams of the headlights. The ladder leaned on the fence, obvious, lumpy, and incriminating.

The five men saw each other as vague shadows behind tree trunks. They all had furrowed brows as their minds raced and their hearts pounded.

There was a metallic unlatching sound, then another; car doors opening. The night was otherwise quiet. The five hiders heard booted feet crunching on gravel and swishing through grass.

Suddenly, a voice rang out in German. Bert nearly jumped out of his skin because the voice was right beside him. *"Komm her, Freund! Saboteurs! Ich habe sie getötet.[12]"*

---

[12] Come here, friend! Saboteurs! I have killed them!

Chapter 16

It slowly diffused into the men's minds that *Quack* had spoken the German words. A trick to disarm the Ottoman soldiers?

"Eh? Saboteurs?" grunted a voice from the direction of the truck. Footsteps came closer. Electric torches played here and there, flashing on boles of trees. But the five hiders crouched low.

"Wo bist du?[13]" wondered a second voice.

He was answered shortly. Bert saw both shadowy figures cross his peripheral vision and said, "Now!" as he leapt toward the nearest.

Confusion erupted. Bert latched onto the rifle of a soldier, and they wrestled with it. Pain lanced through Bert's injured shoulder. He managed to hold on for another second, and then Quack was there, slugging away with desperate strength.

A few yards away, Gooper wrapped massive arms around a soldier and squeezed. The man squeaked as air gushed from his lungs, but he was unable to breathe in again. His rifle dropped to the ground. Tombstone picked it up and rammed its stock into the soldier's head.

Among gusty breaths, voices crisscrossed.

"This one's out cold."

---

[13] Where are you?

"Quack, you could have warned us! My heart stopped beating, I swear."

"Everybody all right?"

"Yes!"

"Yup."

"Aye."

"Yah. Let's get over the fence to … oh, no!"

A metal door slammed. In a moment, the engine of the truck revved.

"There was a third guy!" said Bert.

Gears clashed. The truck spun out. Its rear tires spitting gravel, the unseen driver ripped a half-circle and accelerated.

The five gave chase, but on foot it seemed hopeless.

"We're done for. They'll raise the alarm in two minutes!" Quack said.

"Let us get Lady Ace and get out of the area!" Sam said.

Just as the truck attained full speed, three distinct pistol shots popped. The headlights on the truck went dark. The truck itself veered to the left. It ran into the perimeter fence. The chain-link fence bulged. The truck slowed, but the fence could not contain it. The truck burst through behind the ordnance bunker and flopped over on its side. Two wheels spun silently in the air.

The momentum of their running took them to the split in the fence. Ace stood in a wide stance, silhouetted next to the bunker. A standard-issue Ottoman army pistol sat cupped in her hands, smoke trailing lazily up into the air from its barrel.

"I hate this," she said. Her voice shook.

Sam squinted at Ace. His brow furrowed in concern.

Tombstone let out a slow whistle of appreciation. "Three shots. One for each headlight, and one for the driver. Perfect."

Quack said, "Now what? Did anybody see us? Did anybody hear?"

They all looked out at the airfield and hangars and barracks beyond. All seemed quiet.

"We have seventeen minutes before the foot patrol comes around. We still have a chance." Ace's voice started weak but finished strong.

Sam's worried expression cleared. He smiled sympathetically at Ace. Tombstone said, "All right. Let's git 'er done."

Ace said, "The ordnance officers are, uh, asleep, but I didn't have time to set the detonator-timer. Quack and Bert, strip the jackets and caps off those officers. I'll wear one. Tombstone, you wear the other. Gooper and Sam, load two bombs back into the bed of the truck. Face the fins forward, face the detonators toward the tailgate. Tombstone, come with me to set the timer."

Ace moved toward the munitions building. The rest followed, getting their jobs done and trying to keep in the shadows.

Bert and Quack dragged the unconscious officers behind the building and out the ragged gash in the fence. They returned carrying Ottoman military jackets and caps. Gooper and Sam found that the biggest bombs came on wheeled racks that were easy to roll onto the truck. They strapped the bombs in place, fins forward, staying low to keep hidden.

When Ace and Tombstone reappeared, they shrugged on the officers' apparel.

Ace said, "Twelve minutes to the next patrol. Now, we'll drive over to the air raid siren nearest the airships. Gooper, Sam, Quack, Bert. Lie in the back, flat. Hide. When this building blows up, we'll start cranking the air raid siren, and then we'll run like mad to airship number two. Two down from the air raid siren, that is. Tombstone, take a rifle."

Ace paused for a wry smile. "Did I forget anything? Such as, it was good knowin' ya?"

Five grins answered her for a split second, but then they were all action. Ace and Tombstone, in officer's coats and hats, climbed in the truck cab. The rest lay tense and flat in the bed of the truck. Ace turned the starter over. The truck's engine rattled to life. Ace shifted into first gear.

As the truck rocked and jostled, Bert stared up at the two fat, grim-looking bombs. "Are those window dressing or are we going to do something with them?"

"They're to stuff down your throat if you don't shut your trap!" Quack said.

"Do not reply, Bert. I will slug you," Sam promised in polite tones.

Chapter 17

The truck tractored forward in first gear. The invaders crept into the Ottoman military base like mice into a barn full of cats. It was the middle of the night, but the sheltering darkness was cut by electric lights that surrounded the buildings. The lights glared brighter as the Allies rumbled nearer. Past the airship hangars, a cluster of buildings surely held barracks full of sleeping soldiers. Sleeping soldiers that Ace and her associates intended to wake with sirens.

Those in the back of the truck saw a vast semicircle slide by, blotting out almost half the sky. The open maw of the airship hangar soared taller than a skyscraper. After the first, there was a second. Mesmerized, they slowly counted to five. Graceful, pointed airship noses towered inside all five hangars. The first two airships were skeletons without skins. The last three seemed airworthy.

Gooper whispered, "She said run to the hangar two down from the siren, roight?"

"Yes, sahib," Sam said.

"This is taking so long! The patrol will see the wrecked truck any second!" Bert rubbed damp palms together.

"I'm more worried somebody will just plain spot us," Quack muttered through gritted teeth.

The truck ground past the last hangar. At long last, it sputtered to a halt. The truck doors opened. Tombstone walked around to the back, trying to act casual. His wrists and half his forearms poked past the cuffs of the ill-fitting officer's coat. "Jes' stay put until th' bombs blow, and then run to—"

Quack stared down their back trail. "Look! A flare. Back at the bunker!" The bright flare arced up over the ordnance storage building.

"The patrol. They raise the alarm. Alas," Sam said.

"Now, jes' you stay put fer a hot minute, there, fellers. I got a feelin' that—" Tombstone was interrupted.

The ordnance building disappeared in a bright ball of fire. The flash of light galvanized them, even as it made their hearts leap into their throats. The four in the bed of the truck scrambled out onto the pavement.

A terrific sonic boom rolled down the tarmac. Bert and Tombstone were knocked off their feet for a moment. The profound thud made their ears ring.

Ace was near the front bumper of the truck, at the large handle of the air raid siren. She threw her weight into cranking it. A reddening, cooling mushroom cloud rose at the opposite end of the field. Secondary explosions flashed. The ominous siren wail rose, a desolate premonition of approaching death. Distant shouts babbled after the echoes of the explosion died.

"Go! Go!" Ace urged.

Hoping all eyes were on the fireball and not on them, the five pelted toward the second airship hangar. After a few more emphatic cranks on the air raid siren, Ace sprinted after.

The siren's wailing voice gradually fell in pitch. The runners huffed in front of the first gigantic airship. Feeling exposed, they ducked one by one into the second hangar. A silver behemoth lurked here, silent and huge. Ace's voice came from behind them: "Get in. Hide up in the gas bags if you can!"

The men pelted on, except Tombstone. He and Ace had had a short talk during the tense ride over in the truck. He stopped just inside the edge of the hangar and unslung his Ottoman-issue rifle. Ace stopped too, looking over his shoulder as sentinel. Tombstone took aim back along the line they had run.

Ace looked critically at distant running figures boiling out of barracks and offices. Where did their attention lie?

"Yes. Do it," Ace said.

Tombstone inhaled. Exhaling in a steady stream, he slowly, slowly squeezed off a shot. His rifle bucked. The twin bombs on the abandoned truck exploded. The truck, the siren, and the corner of the first hangar were obliterated by the blast. The illusion held. A bomb falling from the sky would cause similar mayhem. The first airship hangar sagged at the corner. It made steely snapping sounds as it began to collapse altogether. Ace did not stay to watch it implode. She grabbed Tombstone by the collar and hauled him off toward the airship.

The air raid siren across the field began its own banshee wail.

The others saw no witnesses nearby in the hangar as they raced to scramble into the front gondola. The door was in the rear, and a retractable stepladder hung down. They swarmed up and inside. After a short passage between rows of tiny cabins, they emerged into the windowed oval of the control cabin. Ace was last. She scooted around a central pillar to the front. She examined the pilot's controls, trying to sear their layout into her memory. She muttered to herself, "Rudder wheel in front. Elevator wheel must be on the side. Eight engines is a lot to handle. Those levers might be chokes. Or throttles."

"Luck, don't fail us now!" Quack muttered.

"Hear the siren? We got 'em believing it!" Bert crowed.

"That was well done, shooting the bombs in the truck!" Quack said.

"People comin'!" Gooper reported, peering out a window.

"Sahibs, I found the way to the gas bags. Up here." Sam led the way up a ladder on the front side of the central pillar. He climbed through a metal trapdoor in the low ceiling into the interior structure of the dirigible itself. Everyone followed. They closed the hatch.

Just in time. The cabin vibrated as booted feet pounded their way inside. Distant motors of airplanes sputtered to life, buzzing in low, musical tones. The air raid siren still wailed.

The exterior noise covered up the sound of the Allies' own heavy breathing. Everyone hunkered down in the near-darkness and exchanged half-seen thumbs-up signals. They crouched on a balsa-wood catwalk that ran lengthwise through geometric rows of billowy bags filled with lifting gas. Gigantic ribs soared around them in curves full of triangular braces.

Sharp voices barked below them. Compressed gas hissed into the bags overhead. One by one, the eight engines of the airship bomber roared to life. With a lurch, the airship moved forward. Six faces grinned from ear to ear at each other.

Urgent buzzings in the distance indicated planes

taking off.

The grins faded as time ticked endlessly on. Finally, the whole dirigible wallowed back and forth a few times. In the new equilibrium the deck was somewhat tilted. They were off the wheels. Ace gave the thumbs-up with a grin.

At that moment, the hatch banged open, surprising the lot of them.

A half-uniformed airman popped up through the square hole. He was chest-high before noticing anything amiss. He halted face to face with Gooper. "*Was?*" said the popeyed man.

"C'mere!" Gooper grinned. The Brit grabbed the airman's shirtfront with one thick fist and punched mightily with the other.

"Aaah!" screamed the man, thrashing wildly.

"Drop him," advised Ace.

Gooper did, helping his downward trajectory with an enthusiastic push. Furthermore, the massive Londoner jumped through after, boots first. The Allies rushed for the opening, and the hatchway rained bodies for a few seconds.

CHAPTER 18

Ace was the last to leap. Last place did not suit her. There were gunshots down there! Screams, yells, and crashing noises added to the confusion. When Ace finally jumped down, she was just in time to see Sam deliver a felling uppercut to the last Ottoman left standing.

Quack was down, clutching his thigh. Blood oozed between his straining fingers.

Tombstone leaned blearily against a stanchion, holding a bleeding head.

Gooper was still on his feet, though fresh red wetnesses stained his brown coverall.

Bert seemed positively chipper as he went about frisking the downed airmen for weapons.

Ace snapped her attention to the windows.

They were only a few feet above the airstrip! A half-dressed mechanic was standing on the ground, squinting back at Ace. His eyes grew round, and he started jumping, yelling, and flapping his arms. Another problem was apparent. They were lazily floating toward the main runway, into a stream of fighter planes lifting into the air.

Ace vaulted into the pilot's seat. She griped, "Why are there eight separate throttles? That's ghastly engineering. Now, this ought to be the ballast release." She cranked a wheel on the control panel.

It squeaked and scraped. And that was all. There was no discernable effect.

Ace huffed, "No ballast? Fine. Then we need more gas. These ought to be the gas valves." She twisted at a row of knobs.

There was the faint sound of hissing. Everyone exchanged tense smiles. Except Gooper. Gooper was making faces at the Ottoman mechanic outside.

The smiles faded. The dirigible sank. Rapidly.

Ace reversed her valve spins. "Well, all right. Those were for descent. These, then!" She twisted a less-conspicuous row of valve-cocks.

"Brace yourselves!" Sam cried.

The dirigible smacked into the ground at an awkward angle. The Allies ricocheted around the metal cabin, gaining new bruises. The Ottoman mechanic on the ground ran in a panic to avoid being crushed. The airship rebounded into the air on a gentle arc.

"Why no lift? Those are all the valves! I'm out of options!" Ace stared around at the controls.

"Hoo, boy." Tombstone's shoulders slumped dejectedly.

"So close. We were so close," Quack said, closing his eyes.

Ace sank to her knees and ripped off a panel underneath the control console. "It looks right. Just pipes and gas valves."

The dirigible bumped down again. After minor jostling, it settled on its wheels. Sam pointed out the window across the field. A half-dozen trucks with gun mounts were kicking up dust, heading for the airship. "They come, my friends. They come swiftly."

Ace's eyes followed the pipes. They ran under the

floor, toward the central pillar. Her eyes followed the upward. She snapped her fingers. "Of course! More bad engineering!"

"Wot?" Gooper said, hypnotized by the approaching trucks.

Ace became a blur of motion. She launched herself at the ladder and ricocheted upward into the curved basket of gas bags.

"Where did she go?" said Quack.

"Why did she go?" said Sam.

Tombstone said nobly, "Hand me a rifle, Gooper. I ain't goin' down easy."

"Wot? Tombstone, these airship blokes didn't have any rifles."

Bert sighed. "Tombstone. You're wearing the rifle on your shoulder still." Bert handed a pistol down to Quack, then fingered his own revolver. He eyed the approaching trucks, now only yards away.

"So many men," mourned Sam.

"And all of them so interested in us," Quack said, swallowing hard.

Sudden, airy, and full-throated, gas gushed in pipes.

The dirigible creaked and strained.

"Ace?" Sam called.

Ace's voice called back, in a lusty, victorious whoop.

The men watched thunderstruck as the ground fell away. The trucks skidded to a stop below them.

Ace lightly landed back in the cabin. She said, "Overcomplicated plumbing. There's a sort of switchyard of gas lines up among the gas bags. I got 'em open, finally."

She leapt to the controls. "Sam! Bert! Get up to the

catwalks and go aft. The bomb bay has two machine guns. See if you can fire them. We're going to have to fight off airplanes before we're free and clear."

Sam and Bert obediently scrambled up and through the hatch. "Why us?" Bert asked Sam as they lurched along the catwalk toward the rear.

"We have escaped the bullets, sahib," Sam said.

"Yeah. So far," Bert replied.

The giant airship soared in stately grace at first, then with ever-increasing verve.

The gondola window made a "tink!" sound and a bullet hole appeared in the glass.

"Rifle shot!" Gooper assessed worriedly. There was another ping. Then it sounded like a hailstorm as the gondola deflected a veritable stream of bullets.

Everyone ducked down.

The radio chose that moment to crackle to life. A voice demanded something incomprehensible due to static.

"A two-way voice radio!" Tombstone said, impressed. "That's first class!"

Ace said, "I'm starting to think they're onto us. At least we're rising quickly now."

Ace gunned all eight engines. Too much. The airship yawed drunkenly. Back along the catwalks, Sam and Bert clung to supports as they tried to walk. Ace continued to experiment with the controls, and the radio continued to chew them out in German.

"Them rifle shots are gettin' wilder. Mebbe we're a smaller target now," Tombstone said.

Brilliant light washed into the gondola, bright as day. Every fixture, every bruise, and every smear of blood leapt into stark realism. Quack frowned at the light, then blinked down at a growing puddle of red centered on himself.

"Wot's that?" Gooper said.

"Searchlights!" Ace gritted through clenched teeth.

Tombstone said, "Durn. That's a complication."

An explosive boom rocked the air.

"Artillery! Aimed at us!" Quack gasped.

The rattatata of machine gun fire and the moan of a banking airplane added to the cacophony.

"We've been 'it!" Gooper bellowed.

Chapter 19

Ace adjusted the controls. "Don't panic. A few strafing runs won't hurt us."

She was somewhat correct. The lifting gas in the bags was not under pressure. A punctured bag might or might not lose lift, depending on where the hole was located. And there were many bags.

Without warning, a giant hand slapped the tail of the dirigible to the left. The rudder control under Ace's hand jerked stingingly. She fought to steady it. The Allied pirates grabbed at supports to keep themselves from falling. Splintering and ripping sounds and another boom throbbed in their ears.

"Cannon hit!" Tombstone yelled.

"Feels like it put a hole in the rudder," Ace said. Gradually, she mastered the buffeting.

Another fighter strafed them! Dangerous sounding splinters and whiplike whisk noises raised the hackles on everyone's necks. Two gondola windows cracked into a spiderweb of fractures. Those in the cabin could see the ghostly shape of the aircraft and orange sparks from its engine exhaust.

"Ow! Nicked again," said Gooper. He clapped a hand to the crook between shoulder and head where most people have necks.

There was answering fire from Sam or Bert, back in the rear gondola. The vibrations thrummed through the floor. Every fifth round was a tracer bullet that left a glowing trail through the sky.

Ace had the hang of the throttles now. She zig-zagged the ponderous craft as best she could. In general, she headed away from Verviers and its lights. "Darkness and altitude are our friends. The warplanes can only get so high."

Quack said faintly, "We walk on sky trails."

Tombstone said, "Tarnation, Quack! Mebbe he's delirious."

Ace glanced back. "Bandage his leg, Tombstone. Tightly. Stop the bleeding."

Distantly, those in the cabin heard a lusty "Yaaaaah!" from Bert and then a steady vibration of machine gun fire. The machine gun fire doubled up. Both Sam and Bert were at it. The steady drone of a fighter engine hiccupped. Ace saw a flame off to her left, level at first, but starting to spiral down and away.

Ace said, "The gunners got one! We're rising fast now. Pretend you're chewing gum. It will equalize the pressure in your eardrums as we rise."

Another shock and a bang rattled the Allies. An artillery shell atomized a part of the outer skin only yards in front of the gondola windows. One of them shattered. Ace ducked her head under an arm, feeling dozens of glass shards slice fabric and skin. The shards sprayed all over inside the gondola in a blast of frigid air.

"Nicked us good there," Tombstone observed.

"Hang on, cowboy! Oi've got yer back," Gooper said.

"You okay, Ace?" Tombstone asked.

"I'm starting to get irritated," said Ace. Pulling out shards of glass would have to wait.

Another plane buzzed by and there was an exchange of machine gun fire. The dirigible jerked and started drifting to the left. The low music of the engines changed tones. That plane, too, caught fire and trailed away from the airship, losing altitude.

Ace's fingers danced, trimming throttles. "We've lost engine six!"

The searchlights still shone brightly on the airship, but there was a change. With blinding swiftness, bright fog engulfed the dirigible. Visibility shrank to inches. The surrounding radiance dimmed. As they rose through the cloud, the ambient light faded to inky black.

They broke through the top of the cloud and entered a new world. Stars twinkled above. Far below, fingerlike searchlight beams swept and groped fruitlessly. The searchlights flashed on buzzing fighter planes and scattered cottony clouds. Artillery boomed, faint and impotent.

The comparative quiet stretched.

Ace scanned out the windows. "We're too high for planes. The searchlights lost us."

Gooper said, "I'm blind! Tombstone, where are yeh?"

For a full minute, the icy high air swirled in the gondola and the engines hummed. Their eyes adjusted to the dim illumination of the stars.

Ace said, "Looks all clear. Gooper, how badly are you hurt? Can you get Sam and Bert?"

Gooper turned from wrapping a bandage around Tombstone's bleeding head. "Ow, I'm fine. A few flesh wounds. I'll run an' get th' trigger 'appy cretins." He tied off Tombstone's bandage and heaved up the ladder.

Quack lay propped up on an unconscious Otto-man. His eyes drifted, unfocused. He smiled gently. "I have walked under the dancing sky."

Tombstone told Quack softly, "You'll be all right, Quack. By gum, Ah owe you my life. I'd've been shot through the head if you hadn't tackled that polecat when ya did." Tombstone looked at Ace. "He'll be all right, won't he?"

"He'll pull through. If you can find some water, get some down him."

Sam, Bert, and Gooper rejoined them in the cabin. Ace eased back on the lift, set the compass heading to northwest, and pegged the engine throttles to cruising speed.

She turned around and surveyed the battered crew, Ottoman bodies, and demolished surroundings. Her lips curved in a satisfied smile. "Tell you what, fellas. You look awful."

"Feel great, though," Bert said.

"Will you tattoo me, so that I may walk the Sky Road?" Quack mumbled.

Ace said, "London has good hospitals. We'll land there. We'll tune this fancy radio to a friendly frequency and tell them we're coming. This bird has the fuel to get us there, if I'm reading the dials right."

Chapter 20

A silent fleet of official RAF cars perturbed mid-morning traffic around Piccadilly Circus. The black cars glided into a roadblock formation. Pedestrians looked on with curiosity at the sudden military activity.

Then they looked up.

The huge oval shadow angled down in stately grace.

The Ottoman insignia on the side made many double-take and gasp.

The dirigible made a gentle landing in front of the Criterion Theater, its punctured tail pointing down Piccadilly Street. Its engines feathered to stillness, one by one, and there was a sighing, gentle hiss of released lifting gas. Soon it was surrounded by a loose circle of curious Londoners and an orderly phalanx of RAF brass.

An ambulance stood by, with medics and a stretcher. A paddy wagon was there too, with military police ready to take prisoners.

Ace looked out the gondola windows. She seemed reluctant to leave the bullet-riddled dirigible.

"Don't tell me yer losin' yer intestinal fortitude now, Ace!" Gooper said.

Ace said, "I don't want attention."

Sam said quietly, "I understand, Lady Ace. I am sorry. I fear you will attract attention, regardless."

"Rats. I've got a feeling I'm going to be sent home." A captured Ottoman on the floor stirred. Ace gazed at him. She spoke from the heart. "I wanted to help the war end. People killing people isn't *right*."

"You have helped, Lady Ace," Sam said.

Bert said, "The war will end, probably sooner now than before. What a caper you just pulled, Ace!"

"Not I alone. Teamwork got us here."

"Cheer up, Ace!" Gooper said, giving her a slap on the shoulder.

"Ow. Glass cuts," Ace replied. But she winked, then laughed and slapped Gooper's shoulder in return. Gooper grinned.

They all looked out the window to watch the growing crowd, even Quack. The blond man had become more lucid after drinking some water Bert had found in the emergency kit. Now he leaned heavily on Bert. Quack said, "I see photographers! I'd like to see the Emperor's face when he reads tomorrow's papers!"

"Ugh. Photographers?" Ace said.

"Ace. You don't have to talk to any reporters," Bert advised.

Tombstone said, "We been pole-vaulting. That moment when you're weightless at the top o' th' arc is amazin', but you can't stay that high for long. Now it's time to hit th' dirt again."

Sam agreed. "We have flown like eagles. Someday, we will fly together again. Yes?"

Ace laughed lightly. "Sounds good! Keep a channel clear of static for me, fellas!"

Flinging the door open, Ace led the way.

The crowd began cheering.

The Times

Est. 1769   **ILLUSTRATED DAILY NEWSPAPER**   Price 5p

Wednesday, October 24, 1917

AIRSHIP IN PICCADILLY

Secret Ottoman Airship Lands In Busy Public Square. In a stunning victory for Allied espionage, an Ottoman dirigible airship was taken from behind enemy lines and delivered to the busy Piccadilly circus in London. "This previously unknown airship class is a long range bomber, capable of delivering many tonnes of explosives," R.A.F. spokesman Lt. R. J. Sully told The Times from the scene. "Study of it will allow for defences to be crafted now rather than later." What the Ottoman Empire hoped would surprise us is now revealed far ahead ofe its intended

Ace pilot Capt. Cecilia Carroway responsible for caper. The pilot that landed the airship has been identified as Capt. Cecilia Carroway, a U.S. officer attached to the R.A.F. French liberation fleet. Beyond confirming her identity, the pilot would not reveal how the airship was stolen or from where. British Army Regular Phileas Locknard told The Times there were six crew members involved before he was taken to Royal Brompton Hospital, along with two others, not including Capt. Carroway. The pilot is listed as missing in action ...

"Unprecedented" Says M.P. C. C. Cumberbatch, Esq., told The Times. "There were five prisoners of war aboard as well. What a coup. Unprecedented. Our country owes a great debt to these brave airmen."

Airship Remains in Picadilly Circus. The crowd-pleasing attraction is causing a sensation in the theatre district. Speculation is rampant as R.A.F. mechanics examine the craft, estimated to be at least 400 feet in length with eight engines and two machine gun emplacements. A large hole in the rudder was evidently the

NOTES ON THE GREAT WAR

The fictional setting of ACE CARROWAY AND THE GREAT WAR draws from real history even though I swap an Ottoman Emperor for a German Kaiser. German Zeppelin airships really were used as long-range bombers that dropped bombs on Paris and London starting in 1915.

As World War I commenced, airplanes were used only for observation. Some unknown pilot decided to toss a grenade at a passing enemy plane, and soon pilots were taking revolvers, grenades, and rifles aloft to do (mostly ineffectual) battle. In 1915, British pilot Vessy Holt fired his revolver at a passing German observation plane and forced it to land in Allied territory; the first aerial battle with a winner and a loser.

The same year, French pilot Roland Garros mounted a machine gun on his plane. In order to keep his propeller undisintegrated, he wrapped metal strips around it. Bullets from the machine gun would ricochet from the metal bands, sometimes in distinctly unintended directions! But most bullets would get through, and Garros quickly shot down five German planes.

The French began calling him "the ace of all pilots," and it soon became tradition to attach the name "ace" to all pilots that shot down five enemies.

In our world, female pilots did not fly combat missions until World War II, so Ace is a little ahead of her time.

What a silly sentence! *Of course* Ace is ahead of her time!

ABOUT THE AUTHOR

Wyoming native Guy Worthey traded spurs and lassos for telescopes and computers when he decided on astrophysics for a day job. Whenever he temporarily escapes the gravitational pull of stars and galaxies, he writes fiction. He lives in Washington state with his violinist wife Diane.

ACKNOWLEDGMENTS

Deep thanks to critical readers in the Palouse Writers Guild and SCBWI Palouse Writers. Thanks to Dr. McCluskey at Washington State University and Dr. Silva at the National Optical Astronomy Observatories for support at key moments in the creative process. Cheeky nods and winks to quirky NaNoWriMo. Humble thanks and appreciation to my family, especially Diane.

The Adventures of Ace Carroway

Book 1
ACE CARROWAY AND THE GREAT WAR

Book 2
ACE CARROWAY AROUND THE WORLD

Book 3
ACE CARROWAY AND THE HANDSOME DEVIL

Book 4
ACE CARROWAY AND THE GROWLING DEATH

guyworthey.net